"You don't strike me as the type of woman who is often afraid."

"I'm not, but I take care of myself. I don't put myself in dangerous situations," D.J. told him.

Quinn leaned toward her. "I'm dangerous."

"You're a known danger and I'm prepared."

"Not possible."

"Want to bet?"

She was bluffing. They both knew that he could take her easily. Yet she faced him fearlessly.

"Tough as nails," he murmured. "It's one of the things I like best about you."

Her eyes widened and her mouth parted. She looked stunned by his statement. Stunned and maybe a little pleased? He couldn't tell.

Another man might have been discouraged or figured she wasn't worth the effort. Quinn knew better. There was something to be said for a woman who was—to quote Shakespeare—"not so easily won."

Quinn _____ He was quotin _____ d it bad.

Dear Reader,

We're delighted to feature Jennifer Mikels, who penned the second story in our multiple-baby-focused series, MANHATTAN MULTIPLES. Jennifer writes, "To me, there's something wonderfully romantic about a doctor-nurse story and about a crush developing into a forever love. In *The Fertility Factor* (#1559), a woman's love touches a man's heart and teaches him that what he thought was impossible is within his reach if he'll trust her enough."

Sherryl Woods continues to captivate us with *Daniel's Desire* (#1555), the conclusion of her celebrated miniseries THE DEVANEYS. When a runaway girl crosses their paths, a hero and heroine reunite despite their tragic past. And don't miss *Prince and Future...Dad?* (#1556), the second book in Christine Rimmer's exciting miniseries VIKING BRIDES, in which a princess experiences a night of passion and gets the surprise of a lifetime! *Quinn's Woman* (#1557), by Susan Mallery is the next in her longtime-favorite HOMETOWN HEARTBREAKERS miniseries. Here, a self-defense expert never expects to find hand-to-heart combat with her rugged instructor....

Return to the latest branch of popular miniseries MONTANA MAVERICKS: THE KINGSLEYS with *Marry Me...Again* (#1558) by Cheryl St.John. This dramatic tale shows a married couple experiencing some emotional bumps—namely that their marriage is invalid! Will they break all ties or rediscover a love that's always been there? Then, *Found in Lost Valley* (#1560) by Laurie Paige, the fourth title in her SEVEN DEVILS miniseries, is about two people with secrets in their pasts, but who can't deny the rising tensions between them!

As you can see, we have a lively batch of stories, delivering diversity and emotion in each romance.

Happy reading!

Sincerely,

Karen Taylor Richman
Senior Editor

Please address questions and book requests to:
Silhouette Reader Service
U.S.: 3010 Walden Ave., P.O. Box 1325, Buffalo, NY 14269
Canadian: P.O. Box 609, Fort Erie, Ont. L2A 5X3

Susan Mallery

QUINN'S WOMAN

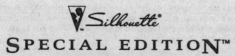

SPECIAL EDITION™

Published by Silhouette Books

America's Publisher of Contemporary Romance

To that young girl who grew up with broken wings,
and somehow learned to fly.
You are, as always, an inspiration.

SILHOUETTE BOOKS

ISBN 0-373-24557-2

QUINN'S WOMAN

Visit Silhouette at www.eHarlequin.com

Printed in U.S.A.

Books by Susan Mallery

SUSAN MALLERY

is the bestselling and award-winning author of over fifty
books for Harlequin and Silhouette Books. She makes her
home in the Pacific Northwest with her handsome prince of
a husband and her two adorable-but-not-bright cats.

Dear Reader,

This is the last book in my HOMETOWN HEARTBREAKERS series. If this is the only one you've read, don't worry—it stands alone. If you've been following the series, I hope you've enjoyed meeting new members of the "Haynes family" and seeing how the clan has expanded.

My original plan was to write two books—Austin's and Travis's. Then I realized there were more brothers who had stories to tell. At one point in time I actually considered killing Craig off and having Jordan adopt his children. I know—a really bad idea. One of my writer friends talked me out of it.☺

When I decided to revisit the series, I had a logistical problem of how to connect these stories with the originals. It had been several years since the last book was out. So I sat down and read them all and came up with the idea of using Earl Haynes.

Okay—for all you who have written and e-mailed to get an update on the Haynes family "baby count" on the original brothers, here it is:

Craig and Jill, three boys from his previous marriage and two girls together. Travis and Elizabeth, one daughter from her previous relationship and three girls together. Jordan and Holly, three girls. Kyle and Sandy, two girls and a boy from her previous marriage and two girls together. Hannah and Nick, three girls. Austin and Rebecca, one adopted son, two boys and one girl.

Happy reading.

Susan Mallery

Chapter One

"Try to bring this one back alive," Sheriff Travis Haynes said as he nodded at the slightly built private waiting by the edge of the makeshift podium.

"Alive I can promise," D.J. Monroe said as she grabbed a rifle from the stack on the table. "In one piece may be more complicated."

The men standing around chuckled, but the private in question blanched. D.J. tossed him the rifle, grabbed a second one for herself, then started walking. She figured her partner for the next fourteen hours would come trotting along as soon as he figured out she wasn't going to wait for him.

Sure enough, in about thirty seconds she heard rapid footsteps on the damp ground.

"What's your name, kid?" she asked when he'd caught up with her.

"Private Ronnie West, ma'am."

She gave him a quick once-over. He was tall—about six-three to her five-nine—skinny and barely shaving. His shock of red hair was bright enough to read by.

"Are you even eighteen, Ronnie?"

"Yes, ma'am. Nearly four months ago."

"You insulted about being paired with a woman?" she asked.

"No, ma'am." His pale-blue eyes widened as he glanced at her. "I'm honored. My sergeant said you were one of the best and that I was damned lucky to get a chance to watch you work." He ducked his head and blushed. "Excuse me for swearing, ma'am."

She stopped walking and turned toward him. The annual war games between the emergency services of Glenwood, California—sheriff's office, fire department and EMT units—and the local Army base were a chance for all concerned to practice, learn and have fun. The morning had been spent on obstacle courses, sharpshooting and tactical planning. D.J. didn't care about any of that. She looked forward to the search and capture phase of the games.

Between now and 6:00 a.m. tomorrow, she and her partner would be expected to bring in up to five enemy prisoners. For the past two years she'd won that section. It was a point of pride with her. The other players grumbled about her good fortune, not understanding it. Especially when she always took a relatively new recruit as her partner.

"Ronnie, let's get some ground rules set up," she said. "You can swear all you want. I doubt you can come up with anything I haven't heard. Or said." She smiled at him. "Fair enough?"

"Yes, ma'am."

"Good. On this mission, I'm in charge. You're here to listen, learn and follow orders. You get in my way, and I'll cut off your ear. Or something you'll miss even more. Understand?"

He swallowed hard, then nodded.

"Last, but most important, you've got a good six inches of height on me and weigh about forty pounds more. Is there any doubt in your mind that I could take you right here, right now?"

His gaze swept over her body from her Army-issue boots, past her camouflage pants and shirt, to her face.

He straightened and squared his shoulders. "No, ma'am."

"As long as we have that straight."

She ducked into the tent her team used for headquarters and picked up her backpack. Ronnie already had his gear with him. When she stepped back out into the misty afternoon, she pulled a knife from the pack and stuck it into her boot.

"Check your weapons," she said.

Ronnie frowned. "They're not loaded."

"Check them, anyway. You always check."

"Yes, ma'am."

He followed her lead and made sure both his side arm and rifle were unloaded. When he'd finished, she pulled her cap lower on her head and wished they could have had sun today. Telling herself the gray skies and low clouds would reduce the risk of shadows didn't make her appreciate the chilly dampness any more. It was nearly July. Shouldn't it be hot?

Northern California weather was frequently uncooperative, she thought as she set off into the forest. Ronnie trailed after her, making enough noise to pass for a musk ox. At least he wasn't a talker. The one from last year had chatted on and on until she'd been forced to grab him from behind and threaten to slit his throat.

Two hours later they were deep in "enemy" territory. She slowed their pace in an effort to keep her boy toy from giving away their position. Her oversize shirt was damp and clinging to her skin, which she hated. Water dripped from her hat. It was the kind of day better spent curled up reading, not combing the backwoods for swaggering men who thought they knew it all. Still, the war games helped keep her sharp. For her life was all about maintaining her edge; the book would have to wait.

Up ahead she sensed more than heard movement. She stopped, as did Ronnie. After silently handing him her backpack and ordering him to wait, she circled around a cluster of trees so that she could come out on the other side.

A man sat on a log, studying a map. She recognized him as a Fern Hill EMT guy. Midthirties, in decent shape, but not much of a challenge. Oh, well, she had to take what she could get.

After deliberately stepping on a fallen branch to make it snap, she retreated into the dripping shadow of a thick tree. The man sprang to his feet and turned toward the sound. His backpack lay on the ground, as did his rifle. He wore his sidearm, but she doubted he knew how to use it.

As the man stepped toward where she'd broken the branch, she circled behind him. When she was less than a foot away, she grabbed his arm, turned him, then swept out her leg to topple him to the ground. He landed hard, with an audible "oof" of air.

She was already on him. After tossing his sidearm into the brush, she turned him and neatly tied his hands behind his back. She was nearly finished with his feet before he'd even gasped breath back into his body.

"Okay, kid," she called. "You can come out now."

Ronnie appeared, carrying her backpack. He stared open-mouthed at the tied man.

"That was so great," he told her. "Really fast and smooth. He never heard you coming."

The EMT guy didn't look amused. "Now what?" he asked.

D.J. smiled. "Now you relax while we search out other prey. I'm not wasting Ronnie's time by having him head back to headquarters with just one guy."

"No way. You can't leave me. It's raining. The ground is wet."

D.J. shrugged. "It's war."

He was still yelling when they were nearly a quarter mile away. She would have liked to tape his mouth, but it violated the rules of the game.

Pity.

An hour later they came upon three men standing together, smoking. They were talking and laughing, obviously unconcerned about the potential for being captured.

D.J. studied the situation, then pulled Ronnie back far enough for them to have a whispered conversation.

"If you want to win, you have to be willing to

do whatever it takes," she said as she slipped off her backpack. "Catch the enemy off guard with the unexpected. I'm going to wait while you get into position. You'll head east and circle around them. When I walk into the clearing, you'll be directly in front of me and behind them. When they're distracted, walk in with your rifle pointed at their backs."

Ronnie nodded, but she saw the doubt in his eyes. He wanted to know how she was going to manage to distract three men at the same time. She smiled. It was so easy.

First she shrugged out of her long-sleeved shirt. Underneath she wore an olive green tank and no bra. Ronnie's eyes widened.

She narrowed her gaze. He blushed, took a step back and stuttered an apology.

While he was busy wondering if she was going to cut off an ear...or something worse...she pulled the tank up to just below her breasts, twisted the fabric into a knot and tucked it against her skin. The stretchy fabric now pulled tight across her breasts and left her midsection bare. Next she loosened the drawstring waist of her pants and rolled them down to her hipbones. She stuck her sidearm into her pants at the small of her back. Last, she dropped her cap to the ground and unfastened the braid. When her long hair was free, she bent at the waist and finger combed the waves in a sexy disarray. She straightened and tossed her head back. Her brown hair went flying.

Ronnie's mouth dropped open. "You're gorgeous," he said, then gasped and quickly retreated. "Sorry, ma'am. I didn't mean to—"

She cut him off with a wave of her hands. "It's fine. Go get in position. I'll give you a two-minute head start."

She waited the promised amount of time, then headed for the group of men. They were still standing around, talking and smoking. She stuck out her chest, then sauntered toward them, trying to look both easy and lost.

"I am *so* turned around," she said in a low voice. "Can any of your gentlemen help me?"

They were all regular Army, officers and seasoned professionals. But they didn't expect to see a half-dressed woman in the woods. It was damp and cold, so she wasn't the least bit surprised when their gazes all locked on her chest.

The oldest man took a step toward her. "What seems to be the problem, ma'am?"

They were all such idiots, she thought happily. They'd left their rifles leaning against a tree. Just one more step and the firearms would be out of reach.

D.J. stuck her hand into her hair and began to twirl a curl around her finger. "This is so not me," she said. "I mean what was I thinking? I don't even remember what team I'm on. I signed up for the games because my boyfriend asked me to, then the jerk dumped me three days ago." She blinked, as if fighting tears. "I'm cold and tired and lonely."

The men moved in for the kill.

"Hold it right there! Arms in the air."

She had to give Ronnie credit. He sounded positively powerful as he gave the order. The men turned toward him. When they looked back, she had her handgun pointed at them.

Two of the officers swore, one laughed. "Hell of a show," he said.

"Thank you."

In a matter of minutes, all three of them were tied up.

The limit for captures was five. There was a bonus for up to four brought in before midnight. The earlier the "enemies" were brought back to camp, the bigger the bonus. D.J. had figured it would take her and Ronnie until at least nine or ten to get four, but they'd gotten lucky.

After the men were tied up, she unrolled her pants back to her waist and loosened her tank top. When she'd collected her gear, she shrugged back into her shirt.

"Don't get dressed on our account," one of the Army officers said with a grin. "Naked suits you."

"How flattering," she said, and turned her back on him. Why did men always assume women were interested in their attentions?

"You remember where the EMT guy is?" she asked Ronnie.

"Yes, ma'am."

"All right. Take these three with you and collect him. After you escort them back to headquarters, make sure they give us our bonus points, then meet me here. I'll be within a quarter mile of this position." She chuckled as she remembered his lack of stealth. "I'm sure I'll hear you coming."

"Yes, ma'am."

D.J. watched as her boy toy led away their prisoners. The officers were only loosely tied together. Rules of engagement required that they cooperate on the trip back in. They were allowed to do whatever it took to get away right up until that first step toward camp. But just in case they decided to give her private the slip, she'd taken down their names.

When she was alone, D.J. sank onto a log and drew her backpack close. The misting had finally stopped. It was nearing sunset, and the day wasn't going to get any warmer. She thought about starting a fire, but that would mean giving away her position. Something she didn't want to do. If no one got too close, she would stay right where she was until Ronnie returned. If she had to hide, she figured the odds of him finding her were close to zero. She would give him two hours to make his way to camp and come back. The return trip would be faster because he would flag down one of the jeeps circling the forest. If he didn't make it in the time she allowed, she would find one more potential prisoner herself and get back into camp by midnight.

Forty-five minutes into the first hour, D.J. heard something. It wasn't footsteps or brush moving. She couldn't actually place the sound, but it made the hairs on her arms stand up and her senses go on alert.

Someone was out there.

She silently slid off the log and into the shadowy protection of a tree trunk. After concealing her pack under some leaves, she confirmed she had her sidearm in place, then set out to find whoever was approaching.

She headed east first, then south to end up behind him. She worked on instinct, still not hearing anything specific, but knowing he was there. There were no bent twigs to give her direction, no footsteps, no startled birds or squirrels.

A couple of times she nearly convinced herself

she'd been imagining the almost-noise and she started to return to her backpack. Then she would shiver, as if someone had raked nails on a chalkboard and she would know he was still out there.

It took her thirty minutes to make the circuit. When she ended up a few yards away from where she'd started, she was disgusted to find the guy pulling her backpack out from its hiding place. He'd gone right to it, as if he'd known it was there from the beginning. How had he done that?

D.J. dismissed the question. Once she verified the man had a purple arm band instead of an orange one like hers, she knew he was fair game. While he was bent over her supplies, obviously distracted, she moved in to attack.

She was less than a foot away when she pressed the barrel of the rifle against his back.

"Bang, you're dead," she said softly. "Now stand up slowly. Ghosts don't move fast."

The man calmly closed her backpack and put his hands in the air. "I heard you crashing around out there. What were you doing? Playing dodge ball with some rabbits?"

She didn't appreciate the question or the smirky tone of voice. For one thing, she knew she'd been quiet. For another, *she* was the one holding the gun.

"Keep your hands up," she said as she eased back far enough to keep him from grabbing the rifle.

When he was standing with his back to her, she considered her situation. The man was tall, a couple of inches over six feet, and well muscled. His stealth told her he wasn't an amateur like many of the participants. Nothing about him was familiar, which meant he was probably Army. Special Forces? Had they sent in a ringer?

She couldn't see his sidearm, which worried her. His rifle was on the ground next to his pack, but where was the handgun?

"How long are we going to stand like this?" he asked conversationally. "Or did you forget the next part? You're supposed to have me turn around, then we eyeball each other. Once you've scared me with your rifle, you tie me up. Can you remember that or should we take it in stages?"

"You have some attitude, son."

"Son?" He chuckled. "Honey, you don't sound all that old yourself."

Arrogant bastard, she thought in annoyance. No doubt he thought because she was a woman, she would be easy to take. She was itching to kick his butt, but she wasn't going to start something before she knew she could finish it. She might be irritated, but she wasn't stupid.

"I have no interest in eyeballing you," she said. "Put your hands on top of your head, then get on your knees."

"But I just stood up," he protested, sounding like a spoiled child being asked to eat his vegetables. "Why don't you figure out what you want first, and then move me around."

She gritted her teeth. "Listen, mister, you—"

He moved with the speed of a cheetah racing in for the kill. One second he was standing with his back to her, and the next he spun in a graceful circle. His foot cracked against the rifle with enough force to send pain shooting up her arm. Involuntarily her fingers released the rifle and it crashed to the ground.

D.J. barely had time to notice. With her arm throbbing, she was at a serious disadvantage. Not that they were going to fight. Her opponent pulled his sidearm out of nowhere and pointed it directly at her head.

Her brain had started processing information the second the man had moved. She knew that he was as powerful as she'd thought, with lethally fast reflexes. He was tall, had dark eyes and the faint smile curving up his lips contrasted with the cold metal in his hand. He was good. She gave him credit for that. But was he good enough? He'd kicked the rifle, not her. Had his mama taught him not to beat up on girls?

In keeping with her philosophy of using every weapon at hand, she decided to find out.

She ignored the gun and drew her throbbing arm up to her chest. With her free hand, she cupped her wrist and forced herself to whimper softly.

Whatever it took to win, she reminded herself even as she hated the thought of appearing weak.

The gun never wavered, but the man took a half step forward. "What? I kicked the rifle, not you."

She glared at him. "Maybe that's what you aimed at, but it's not what you hit." She sucked in a breath and bit her lower lip. "I think my wrist is broken."

He frowned. "I didn't hit your wrist."

She glared at him. "Right. Because in those boots you're wearing you could feel exactly what you connected with. My mistake."

Mentally she crossed her fingers, then nearly crowed with delight as he glanced down at his boots. One nanosecond of inattention was all she needed.

D.J. lashed out with her foot, connecting firmly

with the man's midsection. Even as all the air rushed out of him, he grabbed for her leg. But she'd anticipated the move, and had already spun away.

The gun disappeared as quickly as it had appeared. He had to be weak from lack of air, but he still moved toward her. D.J. prepared for his attack, but when it came, she barely saw movement before she found herself tumbling onto the wet ground.

Part of her brain tried to figure out what exactly he'd done, while the rest of her recognized that the lack of pain anywhere meant he'd held back. He'd upended her with enough contact to send her tumbling but not enough to cause pain. How did he have that much control?

She wanted to summon up a little righteous indignation. How dare he treat her differently because she was female? But she was too busy scrambling to her feet and trying to figure out what he was going to do next.

D.J. crouched and cleared her mind. With a deep breath, she centered herself and knew she had to attack rather than wait to be bested.

As she moved toward him, she saw his arm push out. She ducked, spun and, instead of kicking at his knee as she'd planned, found herself slipping on the wet leaves. Something glinted and she instinctively reached out. Her fingers closed around his gun. He knocked her forearm with his hand so the gun went tumbling. She managed to kick it with a foot, sending it back into the air. With a graceful pirouette, she caught it and started to turn toward him. He ducked, her foot slipped again, and she began to fall. Her right hand shot out, and she accidentally brought the gun down hard on the back of his head. He fell like a stone.

Her first thought was that he was dead. Then she saw the steady rise and fall of his chest. Her second thought was that she had better get him tied up while he was unconscious, because it sure as hell wasn't going to happen when he came to.

Chapter Two

Quinn regained consciousness several seconds before he opened his eyes. He quickly registered the fact that he was lying on his back in the mud with his hands tied behind him. He silently swore in disgust. He'd been downed, not by superior training or force but by dumb luck. Wasn't that always the way?

Worse, the woman had tied him up while he'd been unconscious. Not that she would have been able to secure him any other way. He gave her points for gutsiness, but none for the lucky head shot.

Now what? He figured he would fake being out for a while, just long enough to make his captor sweat his condition. But before he could put his plan into action, he felt a hand settle on his ankle. His interest piqued—no way was he going to miss any part of a show—he opened his eyes.

The sun had gone down, but there was plenty of light from the small battery-operated lantern she'd set on the ground. He wasn't sure why she was willing to risk the light, but he appreciated being able to see what she was doing.

The woman crouched beside him. She felt along the inside of his left ankle and pulled out the knife he'd slipped into his boot. He turned his head and saw she'd already removed the one he'd tucked into his utility belt.

She ran her hand along the inside of his leg to the knee, then down the outside to his boot. After repeating the procedure on the other leg, she shifted and pressed her palm along the length of his thigh. When she'd nearly reached the good part, he grinned.

"A little to the left," he said.

She glanced up. Sometime in their scuffle, her hat had fallen off. He registered long dark hair pulled back in a braid, brown eyes, a well-shaped mouth and a sprinkling of freckles on slightly tanned skin. Pretty, he thought absently. No, more than pretty. She was both elegant and tough. An intriguing combination.

One of her well-shaped eyebrows rose slightly. "A little to the left?" she repeated, then slid her hand over his groin and patted him. "I know most men like to think of their equipment as a weapon, but it's not all that interesting to me."

He chuckled. "You say that now, with me tied up and at your mercy."

"Uh-huh. Just so we're clear, there are no circumstances that would change my mind."

She rose, stepped over to his other side and crouched again, this time running her hands over his other thigh. From there she felt her way up his stomach to his chest.

He liked the feel of her hands on his body. She moved quickly enough to show she really wasn't interested, but thoroughly enough to find any concealed weapons. Or so she thought.

When she'd finished going through his jacket pockets and checking the hem and lining, she sat back on her heels. "You seem to be disarmed."

"What about taking off my shirt?" he asked. "I might have something taped to my skin."

"If you do, you won't be getting to it anytime soon, will you?" She tapped his upper arm. "I tie a mean knot."

He'd already figured that out. Pulling against the ropes hadn't loosened them at all. He was going to have to find a different way to escape. Not that he wanted to go anywhere this second. His captor was the most entertainment he'd had in months.

He swept his gaze over her chest, lingering long enough on her breasts to make her shoulders stiffen. Then he returned his attention to her face. Her eyes narrowed and her mouth thinned, but she didn't complain. Somewhere along the way, she'd learned the rules—if she was going to play in a man's world, she would have to live by male rules. But that didn't mean she had to like them.

They stared at each other, a minor contest of wills. Quinn knew he could wear her down even-

tually, but decided on something more interesting.
A challenge.

"You cheated," he said softly.

He waited for the blink, the blush, the guilt. Instead she only shrugged. "I won."

"You took advantage of an accident."

"Exactly." She shifted until she was seated next to him. "Would you have done things any differently?"

He wouldn't have needed an accident to win, but there was no point in saying that to her. She already knew.

"Besides," she continued, "that was my only chance to tie you up. You wouldn't have allowed it otherwise."

"Good point."

"So who are you?" she asked.

"Your prisoner of war. Do you plan to abuse me?"

One corner of her mouth twitched. "Stop sounding so hopeful. You're perfectly safe."

"Darn."

The twitch threatened to turn into a smile, but she managed to control it. When her expression was serious again, she said, "You never answered the question."

"I know."

She wanted to know who he was, and he would tell her…in time. Right now, despite the cool evening and the damp mud, he was enjoying himself. He had thought the war games would be boring and without any challenge. He was glad to be wrong.

She drew one knee up to her chest and leaned toward him. "If you won't tell me your name, at least tell me why you looked down. You're a good fighter. You had to know it was a mistake.''

A good fighter? Now it was his turn to hold in a smile. He was a whole hell of a lot more than that. She'd never stood a chance, and he would guess she knew enough to figure that out.

Her chin jutted out at an angle that was pure pride. Who was she? Military?

''I knew you were setting me up and I wanted to see what you would do,'' he said.

She stiffened. ''You were testing me?''

''More like playing with you.''

Her breath caught in an audible hiss. Dark eyes narrowed again and he had a feeling she was itching to draw blood.

''Quinn Reynolds,'' he said to distract her. ''Now that you've felt me up and all, we should probably be on a first-name basis with each other.''

She ignored the bait. ''So you won't tell me when I ask, but you'll share the information on your terms?''

''Something like that.'' He figured she wasn't going to offer her name, so he changed the subject. ''Where's *your* partner?'' he asked.

''He'll be back any minute, and then we'll take you to headquarters. He took in our first four prisoners. Where's your partner?''

''I got here too late to be matched up with anyone. Besides, I prefer to work alone.''

''Of course you do.'' She sounded mildly amused. ''You macho paramilitary types always do.''

''That's more than a little judgmental.''

''It's accurate.''

Quinn couldn't argue with that. Instead he glanced up toward the damp, gray sky. "The rain's going to start up again. If you're not going to march me back to headquarters anytime soon, you could at least drag me under some cover."

She, too, glanced at the sky, but in the darkness, there wasn't much to see. He half expected her to leave him in the mud, but she surprised him by getting a tarp out of her backpack and spreading it under a nearby tree. Then she grabbed him under his arms and dragged him onto it.

Her strength impressed him, while her expression of annoyance amused him. What had her panties in a bunch? That her partner wasn't back yet? That they both knew he was better than she was and probably only her prisoner for as long as it suited him?

"So what are you?" he asked. "Not military."

She sat cross-legged on the edge of the tarp. "How can you be sure?"

"Am I wrong?"

She shook her head.

Just then the skies opened. Rain pounded the ground. In a matter of seconds the place where he'd been lying became a puddle. He pulled his knees toward his chest to get his feet out of the deluge.

His captor looked annoyed. He could hear her thoughts from here. How had he known it was about to rain? Who was this guy? Although he guessed she probably wasn't using the word *guy* in her mind. No doubt she'd chosen something more colorful.

"If you're not going to tell me your name," he said, "I can try to guess."

She adjusted the lantern and ignored him.

"Brenda," he said.

She didn't blink.

"Bambi? Heather? Chloe? Annie? Sarah? Destiny? Chastity?"

She sighed. "D.J."

He wanted to know what the initials stood for but didn't ask. She would be expecting that. Instead he said, "I'd offer to shake hands, but I'm all tied up at the moment."

She smiled. "I can see that."

Hey—a sense of humor. He liked that. A rough, tough woman in a very feminine package. If he could just get her to give him another full body search, his evening would be complete.

D.J. glanced at her watch and knew that her boy toy wasn't going to make his way back to her anytime soon. It had been nearly four hours since Ronnie had left. He was either lost or captured. If he was close, she would hear him thrashing around in the bush. The silence told her she was very much alone with her prisoner.

She turned her attention back to Quinn. For a man who'd been left tied up on the ground for a couple of hours, he looked surprisingly relaxed. The rain had stopped, but it was still cool and damp. She shivered slightly. She would like nothing more than to head back to camp. There was only one thing stopping her…one very tall, very strong, very *male* thing.

"The rules of engagement state that a prisoner may do whatever he can to escape," she said. "However, once he and his captor start back to headquarters, he must go quietly."

Quinn nodded. "I heard that, too."

"And?"

He shrugged. "I was never one to follow the rules."

Just what she'd thought. With Ronnie helping her, she might have a shot at keeping possession of Quinn. But with only herself to guard him, he would get away. She hated to admit that, but it was true. He was too good.

She eyed his powerful body and wondered who and what he was. How much did he know that she didn't? Where had he learned it? She'd never met anyone like him, and being around him made her want to ask a million questions. Not that she would. Showing interest meant tipping her hand—something she'd learned never to do.

"If you won't cooperate, we're stuck here until morning," she said. "We'll be picked up by one of the patrols."

"Fair enough—I don't have to take a midnight hike, and you get credit for my capture."

She didn't trust his easy agreement. He was the kind of man who always had a plan. Still, he hadn't made any moves to get away…at least not yet.

He shifted so that he was more sitting than lying, leaning against the base of the tree. Then he jerked his chin toward her backpack.

"If we're stuck out here for the night, how about something to eat?"

At his words, her stomach growled. She hadn't eaten since breakfast. A flurry of phone calls had kept her from grabbing lunch before she'd headed out to the afternoon start of the war games.

She reached for her pack, then paused. "Where's your gear?" she asked.

"Hidden."

Hers had been hidden, too, right up until he'd found it. She wondered if she would be able to locate his pack, then decided it wasn't worth facing the cold, rainy night to find out. They could get by on what she had.

She dug out four granola bars, two chocolate bars, an apple and another water bottle.

"No fast food?" he asked. "I have a hankering for some fries."

"You'll have to wait until they show up on the prison menu," she said as she divided the wrapped snacks into two equal piles.

He eyed the food, then shrugged. "That beats an MRE."

Meals ready to eat. Prepackaged food soldiers could carry into combat. She'd tried a couple and, while they weren't as bad as everyone claimed, she would rather dine on what she had in her pack.

"So you're military?" she asked.

"Sort of."

"Special Forces?"

"Something like that."

She wasn't sure if he was being coy to annoy her or because he couldn't talk about what he did for a living.

She poured some water from the new bottle into the one she'd been using. When there was an equal amount in both, she propped one up next to Quinn. He half turned away from her, exposing his bound wrists.

"Want to cut me loose so I can eat?" he asked.

She chuckled. "Not even on a bet."

He rolled back into a seated position. "Then you're going to have to feed me yourself."

He didn't look very upset at the prospect. In fact, there was definite amusement in his dark eyes.

She ignored it, along with the teasing tone of his voice. If he thought hand feeding him was going to fluster her, he was in for a shock.

"I haven't seen you around town before," she said as she unwrapped the first granola bar in his pile. "You're not stationed at the base here, are you?"

"No. I flew into the country day before yesterday and got to Glenwood this morning. I'm here to meet up with my brother."

She broke the granola bar into small pieces and offered him the first one. He didn't bother leaning forward, which meant she had to stretch her arm out across his body. When her fingers were practically touching his mouth, he finally opened and bit down on the food.

He winked. "The ambiance needs a little work, but I can't complain about the service."

She ignored him. "Where did you fly in from?"

"The Middle East."

There was something about the way he answered the question that made her think she wasn't likely to get any more information from him. She waited until he'd finished chewing, then offered another piece of the bar.

"What about you?" he asked when he'd finished chewing. "You live in Glenwood?"

"Yes."

"What do you do?"

She hesitated because her natural inclination was

to not reveal any personal information. Quinn waited, his expression interested, his body relaxed. Finally she shrugged and gave him the bare-bone facts.

"I'm a private consultant," she said. "I teach classes at local schools, telling kids how to stay safe. I teach women basic self-defense. I'm also on call with several state and federal organizations, along with some private firms. They bring me in to help in extracting children from dangerous situations."

"Domestic abductions?" he asked.

"Sometimes." Domestic abductions meant the kidnapping of a child by the noncustodial parent. "Sometimes it's a straight kidnapping for money or revenge."

She stopped talking the second she realized she wanted Quinn to be impressed. Don't be an idiot, she told herself. What did she care what this guy thought of her?

She fed him the last of the granola bar then unwrapped one for herself.

"Is there a Mr. D.J.?" he asked.

"No."

"Just no?" Quinn raised his eyebrows. "A former Mr. D.J., then?"

"Not even close."

"Why not? A pretty woman like you should be married."

She laughed. "You sound like an Italian grandma. I have no interest in getting married. It was an institution invented by men to get their needs met. They get full-time live-in help, including a maid and a nanny when they have kids. Not only don't they have to pay for it, but most wives will do all that *and* go get a job. Marriage is a great deal for men, but what do women get out of it?''

"Safety. Security."

"Right. Tell that to the women at the local shelter. The ones who have been beat up by their loving husbands."

"You've obviously thought this through," he said.

"It didn't take long."

She finished her granola bar and opened his second one.

"So you keep your men on a short leash?"

She leaned toward him. "I keep them in a cage."

She'd thought he might be offended by her opinions and bluntness, but instead he laughed. Her forearm brushed his chest, and she felt the rumble of his amusement.

His dark gaze locked with hers. "Do you have them all running scared or are a few of them brave enough to stand up to you?"

"Most are too busy heading for the hills. They want soft, gentle, trusting women."

"You can be soft."

"Right. That's me. A delicate flower."

"You're still a woman, D.J. Combat boots and a few fancy moves don't change that."

She thought of herself as competent and independent. Not soft. Soft implied weak. "My moves aren't fancy and I have more than a few of them."

"Tough talk for a girl."

She held up the piece of the granola bar. "Do you want to eat this, or do you want to keep flapping your lips?"

He obligingly opened his mouth. She moved

closer. This time, though, as he took the food, his lip came in contact with her fingertips.

There was a flash of heat where their skin touched, along with a flicker of tightness in her stomach. D.J. nearly jumped in surprise. What on earth was that? She didn't react to men. Not now, not ever. She liked some, disliked others and rarely trusted any of them.

Unsettled, but determined not to show it, she continued to feed him the granola bar but was careful to make sure there wasn't anymore contact. As she finished her second bar, she tried to analyze what was going on. Okay, Quinn wasn't like most men she met. He was unfazed by her or by being tied up. He was an excellent fighter, probably in Special Forces and most likely stationed overseas. He was—

Tall, dark and good-looking. Of course.

Relief coursed through her as she realized what was going on. Quinn Reynolds reminded her of the Haynes brothers. All four of them shared the same general physique, dark coloring and facial structure. She'd known Travis Haynes, the sheriff, and Kyle Haynes, one of the deputies, since she'd first moved to Glenwood. Over the past few years, she'd met the other brothers.

They were all good guys, and some of the very few men she trusted. Quinn looked enough like them to put her off balance.

Having solved the problem, D.J. relaxed. She fed Quinn his chocolate bar, ate her own, then used her penknife to cut the apple in two, then divide it into slices.

"I don't think your partner is coming back," he said conversationally.

D.J. glanced at her watch, then nodded in agreement. "Ronnie wasn't really good in the woods," she admitted. "I'm guessing he's lost. Or captured by an enemy."

"Are you sure you didn't leave him tied up somewhere?"

She grinned. "He and I were partners. I would never actually hurt him. I settled on threatening him."

"Was he scared?"

"Terrified. Barely eighteen and a new recruit. But he knew how to follow orders. We captured four prisoners in our first couple of hours. Three of them were army officers."

"How?"

She explained about distracting them while Ronnie sneaked up from behind. When she'd finished, Quinn shook his head.

"Do you always do whatever it takes to win?"

"I do whatever it takes to be in control. There's a difference."

He glanced down at her hand. "So I didn't kick you in the wrist before. You were faking it."

"Of course."

"I can respect that."

While they were discussing recent history...
"How did you throw me without hurting me?" she asked. "I barely felt anything."

"I have great hands."

She rolled her eyes. "I'm serious."

"I am, too. Besides, I don't beat up on women."

With his abilities, he could beat up on anyone he wanted.

"Being female can give you an advantage," he

said. "Men aren't always expecting women to be tough. Do you ever get into trouble using your femininity in a situation? Ever take on more than you bargained for?"

"I don't go in blind, so no. I'm prepared for every eventuality."

"Do you ever get personally involved?"

"Not even close."

He considered her answer. "You could do undercover work."

"Maybe." But it wasn't her style. "That would require a level of vulnerability I don't allow."

"Sometimes it comes with the territory. Aren't you the one willing to do whatever it takes to win?"

"No. To be in control." She studied him. "What about you? Do you ever go undercover?"

"Sometimes. Mostly I just creep around in the dark, waiting to pull people out of places they're not supposed to be."

Probably a simplistic version of his work, but one that made her want to ask a lot more questions. Doubtful that he would answer them, she checked her watch. It was after eleven.

"Are you going to get in trouble for staying out all night?" he asked.

"Are you?"

"I hope so." He shifted so that he was stretched out on the tarp. "If you're going to make me stay out in the rain, the least you can do is cuddle close so we can stay warm."

"I don't think so."

"That's the woman in you talking."

She started to protest, then realized he was right. The temperature was cool enough to make her shiver. Neither of them would get any sleep unless they could warm up. But stretching out next to a strange man wasn't her idea of a good time.

"Shy?" he asked cheerfully.

She ignored him and slid closer. While she'd "slept" with a few men, she'd never been one for spending the night. She certainly never allowed herself to fall asleep after. Of course, in this case Quinn wasn't a lover—he was her prisoner. That changed the dynamics.

He was big and tall and as she moved next to him, she could feel his heat.

"I could use a pillow," he said.

"Fine."

She grabbed the pack and shoved it under his head. He smiled at her.

"Thanks."

"You're welcome. Now go to sleep." She reached to turn off the lantern, but before she could, he spoke again.

"I can't. My arms hurt."

She glared at him. With them both lying down, his face was fairly close to hers. She could see the stubble on his jaw and the length of his dark lashes.

"I'm not untying you," she told him. "If you promise to behave, I'll take you into camp."

His mouth turned up at the corners. "I almost never behave."

"Why is that not a surprise?"

She reached behind her and clicked off the lantern, then shifted close to him. But somehow he'd managed to move just enough so that when she lowered her head, she found it resting on his shoulder.

Her first instinct was to bolt for safety. Because

she didn't want him to know she was rattled, she forced herself to stay in place. A few minutes later, her apprehension faded. Quinn was tied up; she was safe.

She deliberately concentrated on slowing her breathing. After a few more minutes she became aware of the not-unpleasant masculine scent of his body. He generated plenty of heat, and she found herself relaxing.

"This is nice," he said into the darkness.

"Hmm."

"Don't I get a kiss good-night?"

Her eyes popped open and she stared into the darkness. A kiss? "No."

He made a low clucking sound. It took her a second to realize he was trying to imitate a chicken.

"Oh, yeah, that's going to work," she said.

"You're tempted," he said, "but nervous. That's okay. I understand. I'm a big, handsome hunky guy who turns you on. But you don't have to be nervous. I'll be gentle."

"You'll be sucking wind."

Obviously, the man didn't have any self-esteem issues. Although she wasn't the least bit concerned about her safety, what *did* make her jittery was the fact that the thought of kissing him was almost appealing.

"You're missing out," he said. "You know, you wouldn't even have to untie me. You could take advantage of me. I wouldn't mind."

"Shut up and go to sleep."

He sighed heavily. "Just one kiss."

"No."

"There doesn't have to be any tongue."

"Gee, thanks for letting me know."

"Come on. You want to. How long will it take?
Then we can go to sleep."

Despite the craziness of what he was saying, D.J.
found herself reaching for the lantern and clicking
it on.

"You're getting on my nerves," she said.

Quinn puckered his lips like a man imitating a
fish. She couldn't help chuckling.

He was big, dangerous, probably trained to kill
and he made her laugh. What was wrong with this
picture?

She sighed. "I want your word that you'll be
quiet and go to sleep. No more conversation, no
more requests."

"I'd cross my heart, but I'm a little tied up right
now."

"Was that a yes?"

"Yes."

She leaned close. One kiss, she told herself. Just
a quick peck good-night. It didn't mean anything.
She wouldn't let it. She was just doing this to shut
him up—not because she was the least bit...
interested.

Her mouth barely touched his. There was the
same flash of heat she'd experienced when her fingers had brushed his lips, and a tightening low in
her belly. She braced herself for an aggressive response from him, but he didn't move. She wasn't
even sure he was breathing.

Slowly she pressed a little harder. Not exactly
deepening the kiss, but not ending it, either. Something warm and liquid poured through her. It made
her thinking fuzzy and her body relax. It made her—

Panic surged as she realized she was actually enjoying the close contact. Temptation, desire, need were all too risky. Too dangerous. She knew better. She'd spent her entire life knowing better.

But she wouldn't let him know she was rattled. Instead of jerking her head back, she broke the kiss slowly, then opened her eyes.

She braced herself for a verbal slam, but Quinn only smiled. Not a victorious smile, but one that said they'd shared something intimate.

No they hadn't, she thought as she turned off the lantern and settled onto the tarp. They'd kissed. So what? People kissed all the time. It didn't mean anything. It never had. She wouldn't let it.

Chapter Three

Quinn awakened sometime before dawn. He recognized the gray light outside the main flap of the large military-issue tent, then he stretched on the cot. The makeshift bed was a hell of a lot more comfortable than the tarp where he'd spent the first part of the night. Of course, then he'd had a sleeping companion. He'd traded the company of an intriguing and beautiful woman for comfort. Not much of a trade.

Memories of the previous evening made him smile. When D.J. woke up and saw he'd escaped, she was going to be spitting nails. Too bad he would miss the show. At least he knew she would come looking for him at camp, demanding to know how he'd done it. He'd made sure of that by leaving his cut ropes coiled up neatly beside her. The message was clear—he'd escaped *and* he'd had a knife that she'd missed. No way would she be able to resist a challenge like that.

Fifteen minutes later he was sipping coffee at one of the tables in the mess tent. He'd spread out the morning paper, but instead of reading, he was watching the main entrance, waiting for a tall, shapely brunette to burst inside and demand an explanation…not to mention retribution.

Instead he saw his brother stroll in. Gage looked around him, saw him and started across the dirt floor.

"You made it," Gage said, and grinned.

Quinn rose and they shook hands, then embraced briefly. After slapping each other on the back and reassuring themselves that each had survived and was well since their last meeting, Quinn glanced at the man who had accompanied Gage.

His brother stepped back. "This is Travis Haynes. He's the local sheriff here."

Quinn shook hands with the man, then frowned when he realized there was something familiar about him. He was sure he and Travis Haynes had never met; Quinn didn't forget faces. Yet there was something that teased at the back of his mind…almost a memory, but not quite.

Travis looked him over, then shook his head. "I'll be damned," he said, then motioned to the table. "We should probably sit down and talk this over."

Curious but not concerned, Quinn settled back in his chair. Gage took a seat across from him with Travis sitting to his right. Gage rested his forearms on the table.

"You're doing okay?" he asked Quinn.

Quinn sipped his coffee. "You have something to say, so say it."

Gage nodded. "I just—"

Travis leaned forward. "I should go. After you two talk we can all get together."

"No." Gage shook his head. "Stay. This concerns you. Besides, if Quinn has some questions, you're the best one to answer them." He returned his attention to Quinn. "Sorry to be so mysterious. I didn't want to tell you in a phone message or a letter. I appreciate you coming here."

Quinn shrugged. His work kept him out of touch with his family for months at a time. Their only way to communicate was to leave a message at a special number and wait for him to get back to them. Sometimes he was able to respond in a few days, but most of time it was weeks or months. Gage had left his first message nearly two months ago. His second, requesting Quinn meet him in Glenwood, had been delivered just as Quinn had returned to the States.

"Have you talked to Mom?" Gage asked.

"A couple of days ago. She said everything was fine." He frowned. Had she been hiding something? Was she sick?

Not surprisingly his brother knew what he was thinking.

"She's okay," Gage told him. "I wondered if she'd mentioned anything…" He leaned back in his chair. "This is harder than I thought."

"Just spit it out."

"Fair enough." Gage stared at him. "Ralph Reynolds isn't our biological father. He and Mom couldn't have kids together. They both wanted them so she got pregnant by another guy. Someone she met in Dallas. His name is Earl Haynes. Travis here is one of his sons. Which makes him our half brother.'' Gage grinned. ''Actually, we have several. It seems there are a lot of Earl Haynes's sons running around the world.''

Quinn heard the words, but at first they didn't have any meaning. Ralph Reynolds not their biological father?

A half-dozen memories flashed through his mind—none of them pleasant. Of his father walking away, of his father telling him he would never be good enough, of his father making it clear over and over that Quinn could never measure up to Gage. Of his father... Not his father? Was it possible?

''I had a hard time with it, too,'' Gage said quietly.

Quinn didn't doubt that. Gage and the old man had been tight. Always. While Quinn couldn't wait to get out of Possum Landing, Gage had stayed and made his life there. He'd been proud to be the fifth generation of Reynoldses in town. He'd become the damn sheriff.

''You're sure?'' he asked.

Gage nodded. ''Mom told me. Back thirty-plus years ago, it was more difficult for infertile couples to get help. Plus our folks didn't have money for expensive treatments. Dad was the one with the problem, not her. Dad—Ralph—came up with a plan for Mom to find someone who looked like him and get pregnant.''

Quinn stiffened. ''That sounds barbaric, even for the old man.''

''She wasn't happy,'' Gage admitted. ''Finally

she agreed and headed up to Dallas. She met Earl Haynes. He was in town attending a convention."

"And nine months later you came along?"

"Yeah." Gage shook his head. "Ralph was happy with his new son, everyone assumed he was the father and things were fine."

Until he'd come along, Quinn thought impassively. He'd long since become immune to dealing with the realities of not being wanted by the man he'd always thought of as his father.

"The following year she went back," Gage continued. "She got pregnant with you. So we're still brothers."

None of this was sinking in, Quinn thought. Nor did it have to. He would deal with it all later. For now, he relaxed in his seat and grinned at Gage.

"Damn, and here I thought I was finally getting rid of you."

His brother punched him in the arm. "No way. I'm still older, better looking and capable of kicking your butt anytime I want."

The latter made Quinn laugh. "Yeah, right." He turned his attention to Travis Haynes. "So you're a sheriff, too?"

"Law enforcement runs in the family. I'm a sheriff. My brother Kyle is a deputy. Craig, the oldest of us four, works for the Fern Hill Police Department, and my half sister, Hannah, is a dispatcher. Jordan is the black sheep—he's a firefighter."

Gage looked at Quinn. "I'm a sheriff and you do your own personal version of keeping the world in line. How much of that was because of the gene pool?"

Quinn had his doubts. "I'm not a fan of destiny."

"That's because there are a few things you still don't know." Gage pushed Quinn's coffee toward him. "Drink up. You're going to need it."

"Why?"

"It seems that Earl didn't just stop at sleeping with our mother. He also—"

Gage was interrupted by a commotion at the door. Quinn turned around and saw D.J. burst into the tent. She glanced around until she saw him. When she did, her brown eyes narrowed and she stalked toward the table.

She was walking, breathing outrage. With her olive-and-khaki clothes, her long dark hair, and a rifle in one hand, she was a female warrior at her most appealing.

A young officer started to cross her path, took one look at her set expression and carefully backed out of the way. Quinn doubted that D.J. even noticed. When she reached the table, she tossed the cut ropes in front of him.

"How the hell did you do it?" she demanded.

Fury spilled from her. Quinn didn't doubt that if she thought she could take him, she would be on him in a heartbeat.

Instead of reacting to her question or her temper, he casually sipped his coffee before pushing out a chair with his foot.

"Have a seat," he said calmly.

She ignored the offer. "I asked you a question."

"I know."

He met her gaze, prepared to wait her out. He wanted to smile but didn't let himself. He wanted to grab her by her hair, haul her close and kiss her until

they were both panting. He didn't do that, either.
Instead he waited.

He wasn't sure how long they would have played
"you blink first." Travis stood and moved between
them, ending the contest. He put his hands on D.J.'s
shoulders and not too gently pushed her into the
chair.

"Take a load off," he said. "I'll get you coffee."

She opened her mouth, then closed it. "Thanks,"
she said, not sounding all that gracious.

When Travis returned, he set the mug in front of
her and sat back into his seat. "I see you've met
Quinn, here. This is his brother, Gage."

D.J. glanced at Gage, nodded and returned her
attention to Quinn. "I want answers."

He made a show of checking his watch. "I
thought you'd be back sooner. You must have slept
in. But after the night we had, I'm not surprised you
were tired."

She half rose from her seat. Quinn expected the
rifle to swing in his direction. But before she could
get physical, Travis started to laugh.

"I don't think so," he said easily. "D.J. would
have chewed you up and spit you out."

Quinn met her gaze and raised his eyebrows.
"I'm not so sure."

If he smirked, she was going to kill him, D.J.
decided. Right there in front of witnesses. Although
she wasn't usually one for reckless behavior, Quinn
had really pissed her off.

She watched him drink his coffee, as if he had all
the time in the world. Which he probably did. He
looked rested, showered and utterly relaxed. She
was tired, dirty and had leaves in her hair. Worse—

he'd escaped. She wanted to know how and she wanted payback.

She refused to acknowledge that some of her temper came from the memory of the brief kiss they'd shared. She still couldn't believe she'd given in and actually kissed him…and *liked* it. Not that she would ever let him know.

"How did you two meet?" Gage asked.

"D.J. got the drop on me during the war games," Quinn told his brother.

Gage, about the same age as Quinn, with the same dark coloring and strong, good-looking features, straightened in surprise. "You're kidding."

"Nope."

Gage's expression turned doubtful, and D.J. didn't blame him. As much as she'd wanted to be the one in charge, Quinn had been in control the entire evening. He'd only let her hold him prisoner for as long as it suited him. She wanted to know why. Even more, she wanted to find out all the things he knew that she didn't.

But how to ask?

As she considered the question, she picked up her coffee and turned to thank Travis for bringing her the mug. It was only then she noticed how much her friend looked like Quinn and Gage. The same general build, the same coloring. Even the shapes of their dark eyes were similar.

"What's going on?" she asked. "Is there some kind of Haynes family look-alike contest going on?"

Travis turned to her and smiled. "Funny you should say that."

* * *

Over breakfast in the mess tent, D.J. listened as Travis and Gage explained their surprising family connection. D.J. was more interested in Quinn's early years than in his being a half brother to the Haynes family. Somehow she couldn't picture a kid from Possum Landing, Texas, growing up to be a dangerous operative, but it had obviously happened.

She picked up a piece of bacon and took a bite just as a tall, thin, very damp young man with flaming red hair walked over to the table.

D.J. looked Ronnie over and sighed. "Did you get lost or captured?" she asked.

He flushed. "Um, both, ma'am."

"I'm assuming you got lost first."

He hung his head. "Yes, ma'am. I apologize for not finding you again."

The men at the table had stopped talking to listen to her conversation. She eyed the eighteen-year-old. He already felt bad about what had happened. There was no point in chewing him out publicly. She'd never been into that sort of thing for sport.

"Mistakes happen," she said. "Go grab some food and coffee."

Ronnie stared at her with wide, uncomprehending eyes. "Ma'am?"

She allowed herself a slight smile. "I'm not cutting off your ears, Private. Go get some breakfast."

He beamed at her. "Yes, ma'am. Right away."

When he was gone, she looked at Travis who sat across from her, then at his brother Kyle. They were both grinning.

"Don't start with me," she warned.

"It's not like you to be a soft touch," Travis said.

"I'm not. The kid tried hard and he screwed up. It happens."

Kyle leaned toward her. "He thinks you're hot."

D.J. rolled her eyes. "Yeah, right. I'm sure I'm going to star in all his dreams for the next fifteen or twenty minutes."

Kyle chuckled.

D.J. ignored him. She scooped up some eggs. After a few seconds, conversation resumed and she was once again listening rather than participating.

Quinn sat at the end of the table. She never directly looked at him, but she was aware of him. Of how he and all the other men seated here were physically so similar.

Craig and Jordan Haynes had arrived and pulled up chairs. Craig was the oldest of the Haynes brothers, Jordan the second youngest. Two fraternal twins, Kevin and Nash Harmon were also a part of their group. D.J. hadn't quite figured out their relationship to the other men. Apparently, when Earl had been in Dallas getting Quinn's mother pregnant, he'd also had his way with the twins' mother. Quinn and Gage had grown up with them as close friends, only recently learning they were in fact half brothers. Everyone at the table but her was part of the Haynes extended family.

She supposed there were some people who would have felt left out, under the circumstances. Not her. She'd been part of a family once, and now lived her life blissfully free of familial obligations.

Keeping her head turned toward Travis as he spoke, D.J. casually glanced to her left. Quinn had finished his breakfast. Now he sat listening, nodding occasionally and not saying much. While he'd been two parts annoying, one part charming and very talkative the previous evening and when she'd first arrived this morning, he'd gotten more quiet as the group had expanded. Didn't he do crowds?

She was about to turn away when Quinn moved slightly and met her gaze. His dark eyes didn't give away what he was thinking, nor did the neutral expression on his face. He could have been trying to decide if he wanted more coffee. Yet she *felt* something crackle between them. A tension. Awareness tightened her skin and made her shiver.

Unfamiliar and too powerful for comfort, the sensations unnerved her. Distraction came in the form of Ronnie returning with his breakfast.

By the time she'd introduced him to everyone and had slid her chair over to make more room, she had convinced herself that she'd only imagined the weird reaction to Quinn.

Travis waited until Ronnie had his mouth full, then grinned at D.J. "So, you didn't win this year."

The kid started to choke.

D.J. scowled at Travis, then pounded Ronnie on the back. When he'd swallowed, he gulped down half his glass of milk and shrank in his seat.

"About me not getting back," he began.

D.J. cut him off with a stern look. "Let it go, kid," she told him. "My streak was bound to run out sooner or later."

"Too bad she wasn't able to capture a prisoner all on her own," Quinn drawled. "No, wait. You *did* have someone, didn't you?"

D.J. ignored him.

Ronnie's eyes widened. "You lost a prisoner?"

Travis chuckled. "Don't go there, son. D.J.'ll take your head off."

Ronnie returned his attention to his breakfast.

D.J. couldn't help glancing at Quinn, who had the nerve to smile at her. Just smile. As if he was happy or something.

Nash Harmon, a six-foot, one-inch testament to Haynes family genes, rose. "I hate to break this up, but I have things to see to this morning."

Kevin, his twin, hooted. "Things? Don't you mean Stephanie?"

Nash smiled. "That's exactly what I mean." He looked over at Quinn. "You probably haven't heard. I recently got engaged. Of course, I'm not the only one. Kevin's planning a wedding for early October, and you already know about Gage."

D.J. noticed that Quinn's gaze settled on his brother. Gage shrugged. "We haven't had time to go into that. I'm getting married, too."

"Congratulations," Quinn said.

"All three of you just recently got engaged?" she asked before she could stop herself. "Is it something in the water?"

Travis rose. "Could be. That'll make you switch to bottled, huh?"

"In a heartbeat." D.J. shook her head. "Married."

She held back saying "yuck" even though it was what she was thinking. In her experience, marriage was all bad for the woman and all good for the man. Okay, the Haynes brothers seemed to have decent relationships. And her friend Rebecca had married a pretty okay guy, but they were exceptions.

It seemed that everyone had a place to be. In a

matter of a couple of minutes, the table had cleared, except for D.J. and Quinn. She expected him to stand up, as well, but he didn't. Instead he sipped his coffee and looked at her.

She told herself this was great. Now she could get her questions answered. The only problem was his steady gaze made her want to shift in her seat. She wouldn't, of course. She would never let him know he could make her feel uncomfortable. Nor would she admit to wanting to know what he was thinking as he watched her.

She resisted the incredibly stupid impulse to touch her hair to make sure it was in place, as if *that* mattered, then turned toward him and decided to just go for it.

"How did you get away?" she asked. "The ropes were cut, but I'd checked you for knives. I'd put yours in the pack, which was out of reach. I checked it this morning and you hadn't opened it. So you had a knife on you somewhere. One that I missed."

She had the sudden thought that someone could have crept into camp and released him, but she dismissed the idea. She knew in her gut Quinn had gotten away all by himself. He'd managed to outsmart her and to do it all while she was sleeping.

Even more annoying, he'd left his jacket draped over her, as if she needed protection from the elements.

"How could you have missed a knife?" he asked, his eyes bright with humor. "You gave me a very thorough and very enjoyable search. If you'd like to check me again…" His voice trailed off.

She ignored the suggestion and the teasing tone of his voice. "Where's the knife?"

She half expected him to insist she come find it. Instead he flipped up the collar of his heavy military-issue shirt, and pulled out a short blade. Not a knife...just the blade.

Of course, she thought, impressed by the ingenuity. No one paid attention to stiff collars. The points were supposed to be that way. All Quinn would need to do was a little shift and shimmy to get his hands in front of his body, then the blade would be within easy reach.

The possibilities intrigued the hell out of her. "What else do you know that I don't?"

Instead of making a smart-ass response, Quinn stood. "This has been great," he said.

She rose and walked toward him. "Wait. I really want to know."

His gaze never left her face, yet everything changed. The teasing was gone, as was the humor. Instead, bone-deep weariness invaded his expression. He knew things, she thought as she involuntarily took a step back. He'd seen and done things no man should experience. His life was about a whole lot more than simply getting people out of places they shouldn't be.

"I'm not playing," she said. "I want to learn what you know. I'm a quick study."

"Why does it matter?"

"Your skills would help me with my work. I want to be better."

"Aren't you good enough to get the job done?"

"Yes, but I want to be better than good enough. I want to be the best."

"There is no best."

Of course there was, she thought. There always

was. She worked her butt off to make sure it was her most of the time.

"I'll pay you," she said.

He smiled then. "Thanks, but I'm not interested. Take care, D.J."

And then he was gone. He simply walked out of the tent without looking back.

She watched him go and decided right then she was going to get him to change his mind. She didn't know how, but she would convince Quinn Reynolds to teach her what he knew. She would be stronger, faster, smarter, and finally the ghosts would be laid to rest.

Two days later D.J. still hadn't come up with a plan. What on earth would a man like Quinn want that she could give him? She'd paced most of the night, and when that hadn't cleared her mind, she'd awakened early for a three-mile run. Now she prowled her back room, pausing occasionally to jab at the punching bag in the corner.

"I can see you're in a temper this morning. Want to talk about it?"

D.J. turned toward the voice and saw Rebecca Lucas standing in the doorway of her workout room. She held a thermos in one hand and a pink bakery box in the other. D.J.'s spirits lightened immediately.

"Danish?" she asked, heading toward her friend.

"Of course. Don't I always bring Danish?"

"You're a good woman."

"I know."

Rebecca led the way to the main office, where

she set the box on the front desk and opened the thermos.

"So what has you all crabby this morning?" she asked as she poured coffee into two mugs. "If you were anyone else, I would swear it was man trouble."

"It is, but not the romantic kind."

Rebecca handed her the coffee. "Too bad. You need a man in your life."

"Right. That would be as useful to me as inheriting a toxic waste dump."

Rebecca tisked softly as she poured more coffee for herself, opened the bakery box and pushed it toward D.J.

D.J. grabbed a napkin, then a cheese Danish. The first bite was heaven. The second, even better. She slowly chewed the flaky, sticky, sweet pastry.

Rebecca took one for herself and nibbled daintily. As usual, all conversation ceased until they'd each downed at least one Danish and felt the kick-start, blood-sugar rush of refined carbohydrates and frosting.

D.J. finished first and licked her fingers. Rebecca dabbed at her mouth with a napkin.

They couldn't be more different, D.J. thought affectionately. Rebecca was all girl, from her long, curly hair to her wardrobe of soft, flowing, floral-print dresses. She wore foolish shoes, delicate jewelry and wouldn't be caught dead in town without makeup.

"You're looking at my dress," Rebecca said when she'd finished her Danish. "You hate it."

"No. It's great."

D.J. studied the light-blue flowers scattered on a

white background, the lace at the edge of the collar and the tight, puffy sleeves, while trying desperately not to wince.

"I just don't understand why you have to dress so...girly."

Rebecca took another Danish. "We don't all need to look as if we'd just come from a sale at the army surplus store. Olive green isn't my color. Besides, Austin likes how I dress."

End of argument, D.J. told herself. If Austin mentioned he would like the rotation of the earth changed, Rebecca would set out to see what she could do to make that happen. She adored her husband past the point of reason. D.J. found the situation palatable only because Austin was a good man—weren't those few and far between?—and he loved his wife just as completely. D.J. believed down to her bones that if someone tried to hurt Rebecca, Austin would rip that person into stamp-size pieces.

Rebecca looked her over, making D.J. aware of her camouflage pants and heavy boots.

"You're expecting a war later?"

"Real funny." D.J. grabbed a second pastry. "So what's going on?"

Rebecca filled her in on the latest escapades of her four children, including David's increasing fascination with cars. "He's going to be a holy terror on the road," Rebecca said, her voice mixed with worry and pride. "He's already poring through Austin's car magazines and giving us suggestions for his sixteenth birthday."

The conversation continued. Rebecca made it a habit to drop in two or three mornings a week. D.J.

enjoyed hearing about her family. As she didn't plan to get married, and doubted she would be a very good single mom, Rebecca's kids were as close to her own as she was going to get.

"I'm having a party next week," Rebecca announced as she poured them each more coffee.

D.J. held up her hands in protest. "No, thanks."

"How can you say that?"

"You have two kinds of parties. One is for couples, which means you're going to set me up with some guy I don't want to meet. The other is a girls-only deal where someone will be trying to sell something I'll find completely useless."

"Cosmetics," Rebecca confirmed. "And they're not useless. I know you're not a big fan of makeup, but you take good care of your skin. This line of skin care is really amazing. Besides, it would be good for you to get out."

"I get out."

"I'm talking about spending some time with normal women."

"I spend time with you."

Rebecca sighed. "Why can't you be more social?"

"It's not my thing."

"So what is your thing?"

D.J. thought of Quinn. He intrigued her. "There was this guy I met during the war games," she said.

Rebecca instantly brightened. "Did he ask you out?"

"It wasn't like that. I captured him, but only because I got lucky. I want him to teach me what he knows."

"Which is what?"

"I'm not sure. I've asked around a little and found out that he works for a secret branch of the military. I'll bet he knows more about killing people than anyone I've met."

Rebecca shuddered. "Not exactly someone you want to have over for dinner. What's the guy's appeal? You don't kill people. You keep them alive."

"The more I know, the better."

Her friend studied her. "You seem very determined. Are you sure this is only about the exchange of knowledge?"

D.J. didn't bother answering. It was a stupid question. Well, maybe not *stupid.* There had been that kiss.

She instantly shoved the memory away. The kiss had been nothing, she told herself. Any reaction she'd felt had been brought on by exhaustion or adrenaline or a spider bite.

"Why does your silence sound so guilty?" Rebecca asked.

D.J. did her best not to squirm. "I have no idea what you're talking about."

"Oh, I believe that." She flicked her long hair over her shoulder and shook her head. "If he's so special, can't you just date him? Does every encounter have to be a battle?"

"I asked him to teach me some things, but he wasn't interested. I even offered to pay him."

"Not exactly the best way to win him over."

"I don't want him to *like* me."

"Why not?"

It was an old conversation and one D.J. wasn't about to start up again. Rebecca had never understood her reluctance to get involved with a man. She didn't get that caring meant vulnerability. Danger lurked in most relationships. Men were bigger, stronger and, for the most part, meaner. Not all of them, of course, but D.J. wasn't taking any chances.

"I don't want a boyfriend, just an instructor," she said. "Don't try to change my mind. Just tell me how to convince him to help me out."

"I will, but under protest. You need a good man in your life."

D.J. rotated her wrist, motioning for Rebecca to get on with it. Her friend smiled impishly.

"There's only one way to get a man to do something he doesn't want to do."

Finally, D.J. thought. Information she could use. "What's that?"

"Give him the one thing he really wants and can't get any other way."

Chapter Four

D.J. hovered in front of the hotel room door. She hated to think of herself as someone who hovered, but there was no other way to describe her actions. She reached up to knock once, then took two steps back and shoved her hands into her jeans pockets.

This was crazy, she told herself. She shouldn't even bother. She wouldn't, either, except she really wanted Quinn to teach her a few tricks. But would he agree?

Rebecca had said to find something he wanted that he couldn't get any other way and offer it to him. Great advice, except she didn't know what would interest him. Except for something he'd mentioned while he'd been her prisoner.

He'd teased her about taking advantage of him, joked about her searching him more thoroughly and had wanted to kiss her. She might not have a date with a different guy every Friday night, but she knew something about the male of the species. The way into a man's frame of reference wasn't through great cooking, witty conversation or a sparkling personality. Nope, guys were more basic than that. Something she thought she could use to her advantage.

She stalked up to the door and raised her hand again. This time she knocked, then wished she hadn't. Planning to make a deal with Quinn was one thing, but going through with it was something else. She didn't usually offer to pay for things with sex. In fact it was something she'd never done. But desperate times called for—

The door opened.

D.J. had already come up with several opening lines. She didn't like to get caught unaware. But all her prep work hadn't prepared her for the impact of seeing Quinn again.

As a rule, a man was a man was a man. A few she liked, a few she wished were dead and the rest rarely made an impact on her life. She considered herself sensible, autonomous and rational. So why did the sight of Quinn standing in the doorway to his hotel room suddenly made her chest go tight?

Nerves, she told herself firmly. She didn't usually allow herself to feel them, but obviously they were bothering her. A few deep breaths and she would be fine. Really.

Quinn stared at her for several seconds, then smiled. As the corners of his mouth turned up, he leaned one forearm against the door frame and shifted his weight to one leg. The other was slightly bent at the knee. He looked relaxed…and predatory. Big, tall, powerful.

His physical resemblance to the Haynes brothers eased some of her tension, but not all of it. He might look like them, but could he be trusted like one of them? Did it matter?

"Afternoon, D.J.," he said. "This is a surprise."

"I'm sure it is."

He studied her, his dark eyes taking in every detail of her appearance. Once again she had the ridiculous urge to make sure no strands of hair had pulled loose from her braid.

She returned the appraisal, checking out his blue short-sleeved shirt tucked into jeans. His feet were bare and his hair tousled. It might be the middle of the afternoon, but he looked as if he'd just gotten out of bed.

He pushed off the door frame and stepped back. The invitation was clear. Come on in.

She stepped into the room, showing a confidence she didn't feel. Familiar statistics filled her mind— the number of women attacked in hotel rooms each year, the number of women date raped in hotel rooms, the number of—

She drew in a deep breath and consciously cleared her mind. Quinn wasn't going to attack her. She'd come here on her own. No one was drunk, no one was going to get hurt. Perspective, she told herself. If nothing else, she could stomp the hell out of him and make her escape. He might have fifty pounds of muscles on her but his bare feet were no match for her heavy boots.

"Have a seat," he said, motioning to a chair by the window.

She took in the plain room, the large bed, a desk with a straight back chair, the low dresser with the television. There weren't any personal effects lying around, with the exception of a hardback mystery propped open on the bed. No pictures, no wallet, no dirty socks.

Instead of taking the seat he offered, she grabbed the chair from the desk and turned it around. She was less than ten feet from the door. When Quinn sat on the edge of the bed, she had an unrestricted escape route to either the door or the window. Not that she planned to need either.

When he was settled, she tried to remember what she'd wanted to say. Somehow she'd forgotten all of her carefully constructed opening lines. So not like her. She would have to improvise.

"I'm impressed by what happened during the war games," she said.

Quinn grinned. "I'm an impressive guy."

She ignored the comment and the smile, not to mention the odd fluttering in her stomach. Had the sub sandwich she'd eaten for lunch not agreed with her?

"I haven't changed my mind," she told him. "I still want you to teach me what you know."

"I haven't change my mind, either. Thanks, but I'm not interested."

"I plan to convince you."

He arched his eyebrows. "How?"

"By any means necessary. I thought we could work out a trade. You give me what I want and I'll give you what you want."

Quinn had been hit on by a lot of women in his time. Some had actually meant it, while a few were just in it for the money. Still, not one of those invitations had surprised him as much as D.J.'s.

Sex for information? Why?

He studied her face, looking for clues. There weren't any, except for a faint tension that told him she was more nervous than she wanted him to know. He lowered his gaze to her body. She wore a tank top and tight jeans. No bra. She looked good enough to start a war. He couldn't say he wasn't tempted, but he had long since learned that nothing in life was easy. People always did things for a reason. What was hers?

"What's so important that you'd offer yourself in trade?" he asked.

She flinched slightly at the question, then quickly brought herself under control. "I don't choose to look at it that way."

So how *did* she look at it? Her reaction told him she hadn't come up with the deal lightly. From their first encounter, he knew she was fearless, determined and always looking for an edge. Her seating choice made that clear. She hadn't taken the more comfortable chair across the room. That seat would have put her at a disadvantage. She wouldn't have had a clear line to the door and she would have lost precious seconds extricating herself from the soft cushions.

So what would make her want to subjugate herself to him just to learn a few moves?

"My work is important to me," she said. "I've told you that I'm often hired to help on cases where children have been kidnapped. I'm trained to go in with the rescue team, be they Federal agents or hired guns. Sometimes those situations get out of hand

and I have to improvise. The more I know, the better I can react, the more kids get saved.''

Uh-huh. Do it for the children, he thought, not impressed or convinced. He didn't doubt she was good, but that wasn't why she was here.

''And that's it?'' he asked.

She shrugged. ''I teach self-defense. My company offers seminars on everything from keeping your children safe to how to survive a mugging. The more I know, the more my students know.''

''You're already well trained enough for what you do,'' he said.

When she started to protest, he cut her off.

''How many black belts do you have?'' he asked.

Her full mouth twisted. ''Three.''

''You can handle guns?''

''Yes, but—''

He cut her off again, this time with a quick shake of his head. He stood and wasn't surprised when she rose as well.

He walked close, then motioned her to step forward. When she reluctantly did so, he circled around her. He studied the muscles in her arms and upper back, the leanness of her hips. He remembered how they'd fought together and what she'd tried on him.

''You've developed your upper body,'' he said, more to himself than to her. ''Women are at a disadvantage there, but you've worked to mitigate that. You're strong, you have stamina, you're well trained. Like I said, you know enough.''

''Not enough to beat you,'' she said.

''I'm unlikely to start kidnapping kids.''

''I want the challenge. You should understand that.''

He understood a lot of things. For one thing, the lady had secrets. But then, so did he.

"You'll never be strong enough," he told her. "There's always going to be someone faster, smarter, better."

"But what you know could give me an edge."

What he knew could haunt her and make her wish she was dead.

He turned away and crossed to the window. She wasn't asking about his world. She didn't want to know stories. She was only interested in his skills.

He glanced down at his hands. Sure, he could teach her dozens of things. Would they be enough? Would they make her feel safe? That depended on her secrets.

The irony of the situation was that he wanted to tell her yes. Not because he believed any of her reasons for why this was important but because there was something about her that intrigued him. She was a fascinating combination of tough and vulnerable. He long ago learned to focus only on work, to never allow himself to be touched by anything or anyone.

Could it be different with D.J.? She'd made him laugh, made him forget who and what he was. She'd made him remember a world that was normal. She was tough enough that he didn't have to watch himself all the time and vulnerable enough to—

He cut off himself in midthought. Wanting her was allowed. Finding her interesting was stupid but understandable. Anything else was a pipe dream and likely to mess with his brain in a way that would cause him to end up dead on his next assignment. No way would he go there.

Yeah, he wanted to help her. But he couldn't make it easy. She would never respect that.

He turned back to her. She kept her expression neutral, but he could see the effort she put into remaining impassive. She wanted to bully him into agreeing, or offer him another tempting deal.

"You're not in good enough shape," he said. "You'd never be able to keep up with me."

D.J. was nothing if not predictable. She immediately bristled and glared at him. "I can handle anything you can."

"Sure." He deliberately sounded unconvinced.

"I'll prove it to you."

Exactly what he wanted.

He pretended to consider her suggestion long past when he'd already decided, then shrugged. "You get one chance. You blow it and it's over."

"Fine."

"We'll start in the morning. Go for a run, then work out. If you can keep up, we'll talk about me teaching you a few things. You fall behind or start complaining, it's over."

Her gaze narrowed. "I don't complain."

"We'll see."

He returned to the bed and took a seat. D.J. settled into her chair and tried not to look pleased. Most people wouldn't notice the slight tug on the corner of her mouth or the flash of determination in her eyes, but he'd been trained to see past the obvious to the nuances hidden below. She'd already decided she was going to blow him away in the morning. She was determined to be good enough to make him eat his words. He couldn't wait.

But first there was the small matter of payment.

"Not sex," he said.

"What?"

"You won't be paying me with sex."

D.J.'s gaze turned suspicious. "Why not?"

He allowed himself to smile. "That would make it too easy."

"So how do you want to get paid?"

"I haven't decided yet, but when I do, you'll be he first to know."

That evening Quinn drove across town to meet his brother at the local bed and breakfast where Gage was staying. He'd offered to reserve a room for Quinn, as well, but Quinn preferred the anonymity of hotels. B and B's required interaction, something he wasn't always good at.

He'd spent most of the previous day with his brother. The two of them had talked about the discovery of new relations. There weren't just new half brothers to consider. There was also a half sister, spouses and children. Each of the Haynes seemed to believe in large families.

The large, extended Haynes clan was a far cry from the world he and Gage had known back in Possum Landing. While the Reynolds family boasted aunts, uncles and cousins, the actual numbers didn't come close to those of the Haynes.

He parked his rental car and walked up the front stairs of the large, restored Victorian house. Gage was waiting for him inside the front parlor. Travis Haynes was with him.

"Hey, Quinn." Gage shook his hand, then slapped him on the back. "You're still in town. I thought you might have to bug out."

"Not this time." Quinn's work required him to be ready to leave at a moment's notice. More than one visit home had been cut short.

He greeted Travis. "If you're here, then who's running Glenwood?"

Travis laughed. "My youngest brother."

The three men settled into the overstuffed sofas in the parlor.

"Quinn, I have to warn you that my wife is already talking about a big family get-together," Travis said. "We've had quite a few since Gage, Nash and Kevin showed up. I figured Elizabeth had it out of her system. But now that you're here, she's worried you're going to feel left out. So brace yourself. We're talking picnics, bowling nights, barbecues, that sort of thing. Wives, kids, dogs and babies."

Quinn figured his brother must have hinted that he wasn't much for socializing. "I can probably muddle through a barbecue or two."

"Good. I'll do my best to keep the plans simple, but honestly, Elizabeth doesn't listen to me. She's always been independent."

He spoke with the confident affection of a man secure in his relationship. Quinn knew Travis had several kids and ties to the community. Gage would be able to relate to a life like that, but for Quinn it was as foreign as life on Mars. He'd turned his back on normal the day he'd accepted his current assignment. At the time, he'd been warned that he was unlikely to ever be able to go back. The job wouldn't stop him, but what he'd seen, what he'd become, would.

At first Quinn hadn't believed them, but now he

knew they were right. He lived in a shadowy world that didn't have room for relationships, caring or commitments. For a long time he hadn't minded, but lately he'd started wondering if there was something else out there. Something beyond staying alive and getting the job done.

"We're all talking about how you got the drop on D.J.," Travis said with a grin. "Last time I saw her, she was still furious about you cutting your ropes and getting away while she was sleeping."

Quinn shrugged. "She was good."

"Not good enough," Travis said. "I don't know what it is you do, but you're well trained."

Trained didn't begin to describe it.

"Who is she?" he asked. "I know she's into teaching women self-defense and keeping kids safe, but where did she get her education?"

Travis raised his eyebrows. "Interesting. The lady was asking about you, too."

The information pleased Quinn. He liked knowing that D.J. had been thinking about him. Had it been as more than just a potential instructor? He remembered her temper, her competence and the soft pressure of her light kiss.

Trouble, he thought. But the best kind.

"Are you interested in her?" Gage asked. "She's nothing like your usual women."

Quinn laughed. "True enough."

Gage looked at Travis. "My brother tends to seek out beautiful women who have nothing to say."

"Maybe I'm not into conversation."

"I know you're not."

"I like to keep things simple."

"D.J. is a lot of things, but not simple and not easy," Travis warned.

"I already figured that out," Quinn told him.

D.J. was a challenge. In the past he hadn't been able to risk that. He couldn't get involved in anything that would last more than a few days. Ties weren't part of the job. After living on the edge of humanity for months at a time, ties became an impossibility.

Were they possible now? Could he remember what it was like to want a woman for more than sex? This was the first time in years he'd sensed possibilities. D.J. might be the only woman he'd ever met he couldn't scare off with the truth. Was that a good thing for either of them?

"She's been in town about four years," Travis told him. "Before that she was in southern California. If you want to know any more background, you're going to have to ask her yourself."

"Fair enough."

Travis leaned forward. "Quinn, you're family. My brothers, Hannah and I are glad you and Gage found us. We want to get to know you better. Our father wasn't one for giving a damn about his kids, so we've learned to look out for each other."

He hesitated, then shrugged. "But I have to be honest. D.J. isn't like other women. She's tough and determined. A hell of a fighter. But inside—I can't explain it. I'm not going to be an idiot and tell you to back off. But I care about her. We all do."

"I understand."

Quinn did. Torn between newly discovered family, and the loyalty that went with that, and his relationship with D.J., Travis didn't want Quinn to use D.J. and dump her.

Gage shook his head. ''Travis, she seems more than capable of taking care of herself.''

''She is.''

But he didn't sound completely convinced. Quinn got that, too. Despite the attitude and the muscles, there was still something vulnerable about D.J. Maybe it was the weight of the chip on her shoulder. Lugging something that large around was bound to slow her down.

Quinn thought about reassuring Travis, but his half brother didn't know him from a rock. Words were meaningless until there were actions to back them up. In time Travis would see that Quinn had no interest in using anyone. He saw D.J. as unique and appealing.

What on earth would Travis say if he knew D.J. had offered sex in exchange for Quinn teaching her what she wanted to know? He had a bad feeling Travis wouldn't believe him, and might even want to take things outside. Not exactly a good way to start a brotherly bond.

No, that information was better left private. Quinn wasn't going to say anything, and he doubted D.J. would be telling the world what she'd done. It would be their little secret...and it reminded him he still had to come up with what he wanted from her in payment. The possibilities were endless.

Travis headed home about an hour later. Quinn glanced at his watch. ''Don't you have a blonde waiting for you upstairs?''

''No. Kari's in San Francisco for a couple of days

visiting a friend of hers. We could grab a bottle of scotch and get drunk.''

Quinn held up his hands. ''Thanks, but I'm not in the mood for a hangover.''

Gage laughed. ''I'm not, either. I guess we're getting old.''

''It was bound to happen.''

His brother stretched out his legs in front of him and rested his hands on his stomach. ''I talked to Mom today. She and John are working out the final details of the wedding. Are you going to be able to get time off?''

''I don't know. I'll do my best.''

''Mom would really like you there.''

''I want to come.''

Quinn figured in the past ten years he'd missed enough holidays and special occasions for three lifetimes. While his father—make that Ralph Reynolds—had been alive, he hadn't minded staying away. But in the past few years, he'd felt a tug to be home.

He studied Gage. They looked enough alike that no would mistake them for anything but brothers. Older by a year, Gage had been the favorite son. A gifted athlete, smart, popular. For a long time Quinn had been right behind him, inching close to his sports records, sometimes beating them. He'd gotten as good grades in most subjects, better in a few, but it hadn't mattered. Not to the man who raised them. In his eyes, Gage could do no wrong and Quinn could do no right.

''You still miss him?'' he asked.

Gage looked at him. ''Dad?''

Quinn nodded.

"Sometimes. Yeah, I guess. I can't think of him as anything but my father." He grimaced. "I did at first. When I found out the truth, I figured I'd lost my whole world. I didn't know who I was or where I belonged."

"Five generations of Reynoldses in Possum Landing," Quinn said.

"Right. I wasn't one of them anymore."

Quinn would consider that a good thing, but he knew his brother wouldn't agree.

"What changed your mind?" he asked.

Gage smiled. "Kari. She pretty much slapped me upside the head and told me to get over it. It didn't take me long to see that she was right. Dad might not have gotten Mom pregnant, but he was still my father in every way that matters." His expression darkened. "Not comforting to you, I know."

Quinn lifted a shoulder. "He was who he was."

"There was a reason he hated you."

Quinn looked at him. "I already figured that out."

"What do you mean?"

"You said they couldn't have kids and that Mom got pregnant by Earl Haynes. That was the deal. But something happened, and she went back the following year. I don't know if she went just to talk to him or if she had something else on her mind. Whatever the reason, she came back pregnant. I'm guessing Ralph didn't appreciate that. You were the son he always wanted. I was the living, breathing reminder of his wife's infidelity."

Gage sat up straight and swore. His reaction, not to mention his stricken expression, told Quinn he'd nailed it in one.

Once he knew the logistics of his mother's pregnancy, the rest hadn't been hard to figure out. Funny how years ago he would have sold his soul to understand how the man he'd thought of as his father could love Gage so much and hate him with equal intensity. He remember being ten and crying himself to sleep. He remembered his mother holding him, trying to convince him that his father *didn't* hate him. He'd begged her to tell him why his father acted the way he did and she never had. How could she?

After all this time, he finally understood, only to realize that knowing the truth didn't change anything. It hadn't mattered then and it still didn't matter.

"I'm sorry," Gage said.

"I wasn't your fault. I'm not sure it was anyone's."

The old man was dead. The past was over. Quinn was more than ready to move on.

"You and Kari set a date yet?" he asked.

Gage hesitated, as if not sure he would accept the change in topic, then he grinned. "New Year's Eve. She says it's because it's romantic, but I think she wants to be sure I never forget."

Quinn had seen his brother with the tall, pretty blonde, and he was surprised they were willing to wait so long to tie the knot. "Why the delay?"

"Mom's wedding. If Kari and I had picked an earlier date, Mom would have cut back on her own plans. She and John want to take a long honeymoon in Australia and neither of us wanted them to cancel. Kari and I have our whole lives together. Waiting a few months won't matter."

Gage sounded like a man sure of his place in the

world. But then, he'd always been like that. He was the one who fit in. Now he'd found the one woman who could make his world complete.

Quinn was pleased. He still remembered his brother's hang-dog expression when Kari had run off eight years ago. Gage had been planning happily-ever-after with a young woman who had a different idea of her future. Yet somehow they'd managed to find each other again.

"You ever think about what would have happened if Kari hadn't left town the first time you two were together?" he asked.

Gage nodded. "I used to think about it all the time. After she came back to Possum Landing, I realized we'd both been too young. I'm not sure we would have made it. This time I know we'll have a long future together."

"Good for you."

His brother looked at him. "I want to ask if there's anyone in your life."

Quinn laughed. "I don't stick around long enough for that to happen."

"Will you ever?"

Stick around? "I've been giving it some thought," he admitted.

"I'm not going to ask you about your job," Gage told him. "If you want to talk, I'm more than willing to listen."

"I appreciate that."

"If you want to talk about Dad, I'll listen to that, too."

Quinn knew the offer was genuine and he appreciated it. But after all these years there wasn't a whole lot left to say.

Chapter Five

D.J. arrived at the park where they'd agreed to meet five minutes before her appointment with Quinn. She'd walked the three blocks from her office, using the time to try to clear her head and focus. She hadn't been all that successful.

Lack of sleep, she told herself as she stretched her legs. Under other circumstances she would say she was on edge. Not this time, though. There was no reason to be. Quinn was just some guy who knew things she wanted to know. Nothing more.

As she bent over to stretch her hamstrings, she pressed her lips together. Okay, maybe, just maybe Quinn got to her in a way that most men didn't. Maybe there was something more to her reaction than simple admiration for his abilities. She pushed her palms to the grass and felt the pull in the backs of her legs. Maybe she found him attractive.

D.J. wasn't entirely comfortable with *that* concept. While she was willing to acknowledge some men were better looking than others, she didn't usually care one way or the other. Any interest she had in their physical nature was more in the lines of their potential threat value. Of course, it didn't matter if she thought Quinn was handsome, right?

She wrapped her arms around her calves and pressed face into her knees, then straightened. And nearly screamed.

Quinn stood less than ten feet away. Somehow he'd approached with such stealth that she'd never heard him. Her heart jumped into overdrive, and sweat broke out on her back. Proof of her vulnerability made her want to back up fifteen feet, but she forced herself to stand her ground.

"Morning," he said with an easy smile. "Ready to kick butt?"

Faking a confidence she didn't feel, she planted her hands on her hips. "As long as it's yours."

"We'll see. You warmed up?"

She nodded.

"Then let's go."

He headed for the jogging trail. She fell into step beside him.

They'd both dressed in shorts and a T-shirt. The morning had started with a light fog, but it would break up quickly, then the temperature would warm. She wasn't sure what he thought of her attire, but she found his slightly distracting. His gym shorts exposed the muscled firmness of his thighs, while the worn T-shirt pulled at his broad shoulders. Once again he reminded her of a predator.

She told herself that the slight tightening in her

stomach was a natural reaction to being around a dangerous animal. It didn't have anything to do with his chiseled body or loose-hipped grace.

D.J. matched Quinn's long-legged stride. As he picked up the pace, she kept her breathing slow and deep. Their feet pounded out a steady rhythm.

"We're going to need to find a gym at the end of the run," he said. "I planned a route that will have us finish up at your office. I figured you'd know the closest place to work out."

How did he know where she worked? Travis or Kyle, she told herself. They knew where her office was located, and they were Quinn's new family.

"I have a weight room in the back of the office," she said as they jogged under several trees. "We can finish up there."

"Great." He shot her a grin and picked up the pace. "Six miles okay by you?"

Six miles? At nearly a run? "Not a problem."

They arrived back at her office in less time than she would have thought possible. D.J. considered herself fit and athletic, but Quinn had continued increasing the speed of their run until she'd been gasping for breath. But she'd kept up and she hadn't complained.

After unlocking the front door, she walked into the empty front office. Her part-time help didn't start until after lunch.

She'd left a six-pack of bottled water on the reception desk. After tossing a bottle to Quinn, she took one for herself and downed about a third of it. She wanted more, but knew she had to wait and let her body cool down a little.

Sweat dripped off her. She'd pulled her hair back into a French braid that morning and the long end was plastered against her T-shirt. She felt hot, flushed and in desperate need of a shower. But there was still part two of the tryout.

"The weight room is back this way," she said, careful to speak slowly so she didn't gasp the words.

By contrast Quinn was breathing evenly, as if the run hadn't winded him at all. He was sweating, but not in any distress. He sipped his water.

She led the way down the short hallway to the big open back room. When she'd rented the office, she'd specifically looked for a location that had space for a workout room. There were mirrors along the rear wall. Weight equipment lined the right side of the room, while thick floor mats defined a sparring area on the left.

D.J. finished her water and tossed the empty plastic bottle into a green bin marked Recycling then faced Quinn.

"Let's do it," she said.

His eyebrows rose. "Why don't you take me through your regular routine?"

She preferred to work out alone, but this wasn't about what she liked. She had to make a point.

She grabbed twenty-pound free weights and started with walking lunges. From there she headed to the machines. Quinn didn't say anything as she went through several exercises, although she could feel him watching her. His silent attention started to get irritating, but it was his physical strength that made her uneasy as he started to work out with her. He could leg press seventy pounds more than she could. After she used a set of weights, he picked them up in one hand as if they weighed nothing. When she went to the barbell for chest presses, adding on enough weight to make her shake through the last set, he stood by her head and spotted her. After she finished, he casually picked up the equipment and slipped it back into place without breathing hard.

Pausing to wipe sweat from her face and neck, she studied him in the mirror. On the run, she'd been too busy trying to keep up to really catalogue the powerful muscles ripping through his body. Now she could see the definition and thickness of his chest and the strength in his legs. He wasn't cut like a gym jockey. Instead his muscles had a purpose. He was the kind of man who knew how to make his living the hard way.

He scared the hell out of her.

D.J. swallowed the fear and kept herself focused through her tricep presses, then leaned back on the bench and exhaled.

"That's it," she said, wondering if she had the strength to stand. Her bones felt as if they'd turned to putty. Her muscles were as resistant as cooked pasta.

"Not bad," he said, holding out his hand.

She glanced from it to his face, then back. She understood the gesture. He was offering to help her to her feet. The logical, rational part of her brain said to save her own strength and accept the assistance. The less-in-control side of her psyche warned her that once he had her hand in his, he could easily flip her and get her in a lock that she could never break.

Deliberately D.J. grabbed his hand and pulled herself up.

Nothing bad happened, unless she counted ending up standing too near to Quinn. They were only inches apart—so close that she could see the various shades of brown and gold that made up the deep color of his irises.

"You work hard," he said. "You're strong and disciplined."

His words pleased her. "Great. So now—"

He cut her off with a smile. "Now let's see what you can do on the mats."

She wanted to groan in protest. She wanted to flop down on the floor and sleep for a week. She wanted a full body massage followed by some time in a sauna. Her legs quivered at the thought of supporting her weight for even one more second.

"Why not?" she said instead and led the way to the sparring mats.

Quinn stood across from her. He was relaxed, his legs slightly bent, his arms at his sides.

"Attack me," he said.

D.J. wished she was big enough so that just sitting on him would squish out all his air. Unfortunately she wasn't, so she was left with no option but to do what he said.

She considered several tactics. Her only chance at something close to a decent showing was to surprise him. She feigned a jab with her right hand, shifted right, made a quarter turn toward him and punched a kick right at his—

Thunk. The floor came sailing up from nowhere as she found herself flat on her back. Now she was not only tired, but sore all over. She scrambled to her feet.

"Again," he said.

She attacked, with no better luck at times two, three and four. On the last tumble to the ground she was too close to the edge of the mat and her elbow connected with the wood floor. Pain exploded with such intensity that she thought she might throw up.

Quinn knelt down next to her. "You okay?"

Speech was impossible, so she nodded. He reached for her arm and probed her elbow. Even the light brush of his fingers made her grit her teeth to keep from gasping.

"Nothing's broken," he told her.

Great. If "not broken" hurt this much she would hate to encounter actual bone shards. She'd had a broken arm as a kid and didn't remember it hurting so badly. She forced herself back to her feet, expecting him to tell her to attack again. Instead he moved in front of her.

"We'll do this one in slow motion," he said. "You start your moves and I'll show you how I counter them."

He took her through the movement step by step until she saw how he had managed to stop her each time.

"Now that you know what I'll be doing, you can respond differently," he said.

"Okay."

"Ready?"

She nodded and moved in. This time when he spun and grabbed for her, she stepped out of reach. Nanoseconds later his leg shot out and connected, an arm moved and she was flipped and sailing onto the mat again. But instead of stepping back as he had before, he moved forward, bending toward her.

D.J. hadn't expected him to get so close. As the air rushed out of her body, her mind blurred at the edges. Quinn disappeared and in his place she saw her father looming over her. She could smell the liquor. People always said that vodka had no odor, but they were wrong. The scent seeped from her father's skin and made her stomach get all tight and sore.

She could see the man's bloodshot eyes, and the angry twist of his mouth. The baseball bat in his hands rose and then slowly sank toward her. She braced herself for the crunch of hard wood against bone and tried not to imagine the pain that would explode when he broke not just her body but her soul.

She blinked and he was gone. There was only Quinn staring down at her, his brown eyes crinkling slightly as he smiled.

"You got the wind knocked out of you," he said. "Can you breathe?"

Could she? She tried an experimental breath and felt air fill her lungs. She felt both hot and cold, as if she'd just broken a fever. She could taste the terror—it was metallic, just like blood.

"You've got potential," Quinn said, as he held out his hand again.

She wanted to run, to scream, to disappear. But she'd long ago learned that the only way to conquer her fear was to face it head-on. She took the hand he offered and let him pull her to her feet.

When she was standing, she resisted the blinding

need to bolt. Instead she crossed to the small refrigerator in the corner and pulled out a bottle of water.

"Want one?" she asked.

"Sure."

She tossed him one, then took hers in her hand. After gulping down half of it, she placed the cool plastic on the back of her neck. Then she walked the length of the exercise room and tried to get calm.

Irrational fear caused a chemical reaction in the body, she reminded herself. The fight-or-flight response was triggered, and her mind was no longer in control.

She was fine. Or if she couldn't believe that, she *would* be fine in just a minute or so.

She walked back and forth three times, then risked glancing at Quinn. He was watching her. While she knew there was no way he could figure out what had just happened, she couldn't help feeling vulnerable and afraid.

Fear. She hated it. Fear was weakness, and the only antidote was to be strong.

She stopped in front of him. "So?"

She made the word a challenge.

"I'll take you on," he said.

She felt both relief and apprehension. She wanted to learn, but why did he have to be the one teaching her?

"Great." She drank the rest of her water. "How long are you going to be in town?"

"A few weeks."

That surprised her. "Don't you have to get back to your assignment, or whatever it is you call it?"

He shrugged. "I'm on leave. Voluntarily. I'll be

around long enough to teach you a few new moves.''

Leave? Why? But she didn't ask. There was a more important question.

''What do you want?''

He twisted the cap off the water bottle and downed the liquid in several long, slow gulps. A single drop escaped from the corner of his mouth. She watched it trail down his jaw to his throat where it blended in with the sweat glistening there. When he'd finished, he turned his dark gaze on her.

''Let's see,'' he said. ''You've offered me money and sex. What else you got?''

The blunt question stunned her. ''You're the one who has to define the price. I decide if I want to pay it.''

''Good point.'' He looked her up and down. ''Okay. Here's the deal. I'll give you the lessons you want. In return, you'll keep me company while I'm in town.''

She relaxed immediately. ''You mean sex.''

''I mean dinner.''

She blinked. ''What?''

''Dinner. It's the meal that comes after lunch. I want you to have dinner with me tonight.''

She took a step back. ''Hell, no'' hovered on her lips, but she sucked in the words.

''One dinner in exchange for teaching me while you're in town?'' she asked.

''We're starting with one dinner. There might be more. I might even want you to join me for lunch.''

She really wanted to say no. Nothing about this appealed to her. For one thing, it didn't make sense.

For another, she hated anything to be open-ended. She wanted the rules defined up front.

"You can pick the restaurant," he said. "This is your town, after all. But nothing cheap. No fast food, no burger places. Somewhere nice. And you have to wear a dress. I want to see cleavage and legs."

She nearly decked him for the last crack. "I don't date."

"This isn't a date. It's business."

He moved close. She braced herself to ward off an attack, but instead he simply tucked a loose strand of hair behind her ear. She found herself wanting to lean into the tender gesture. So, of course, she didn't.

"I've been out of the country a long time," he said. "Is it so hard to believe I want to have dinner with a beautiful woman?"

She nearly spit in surprise. "Somewhat attractive" she would have bought, but beautiful?

"I don't play boy-girl games," she said. "They're all designed to make sure the boys win."

"I'm not a boy."

There was a news flash. She narrowed her gaze.

He grinned. "Dinner in exchange for lessons. What's not to like?"

She wanted to throw his offer back in his face but couldn't say why. What was the big deal about having dinner? Logically it was easier than having sex with him. Except sex was little more than a bodily function. She could disconnect and it wouldn't matter. Dinner...dinner was complicated.

"Fine," she ground out as she clenched her teeth. "Dinner."

"I'll pick you up at seven."

"No, I'll come get you at your hotel."

"Works for me."

She glanced at the wall clock. "You probably have to be somewhere, huh?"

He laughed. "Subtle, D.J., real subtle."

He made no move to leave.

"I have to get to work," she said. "I have a business to run."

"Fair enough. Just answer one question."

She braced herself, knowing she wasn't going to like it. "What?"

"Why did going out to dinner with me throw you more than what you'd offered before?"

She might have known he would see her discomfort. She searched for a good lie, but couldn't find one. Which left the truth.

"Sex is easy because it doesn't matter."

His expression didn't change. "It can."

"Has it ever for you? Even once?"

He hesitated. "Maybe a few times."

"Sure. It's that way for guys. Why does it have to be different for me?"

He studied her face. "I guess it doesn't. See you tonight."

He walked out of the room and headed for the office. When the front door closed behind him, D.J. breathed out a sigh of relief. That was over.

Except it wasn't. Even though Quinn had physically left the office, she couldn't stop thinking about him. When she thought about their dinner that night, she felt an odd combination of apprehension and anticipation.

Crazy, she told herself. She barely knew the man.

He didn't matter in any significant way. Nor was he ever going to. Letting a man get close was a recipe for disaster.

With a shiver, she remembered the flashback she'd had of her father. Cold seeped into her, but she ignored it. He was long since dead and she'd never spent a single day mourning the loss. She refused to waste another minute thinking about him now.

D.J. felt like an idiot…probably because she looked like one.

She sat in front of the mirror and fingered the curlers in her hair. Rebecca lightly slapped away her hand.

"You'll mess up my hard work. Now try the darker lipstick."

D.J. dutifully picked up the tube Rebecca gave her and applied the color over the medium pink she'd already put on. When she was finished, she waited for her friend's pronouncement.

Rebecca tilted her head and wrinkled her nose. "Better, but not perfect."

"It's lipstick. It doesn't *have* to be perfect."

Rebecca muttered something under her breath and reached for another tube from the bag she'd dragged over. While she searched for the right shade, D.J. studied her reflection in the mirror and wondered— for the seven hundred and fifty-second time—why she'd agreed to the date.

Not a date, she reminded herself. Payment. Unfortunately the definition clarification didn't make her feel any better about what she was doing. The smoky eye shadow and dark mascara didn't help, either. Makeup, jewelry and high heels were typical female trappings she generally avoided for an assortment of reasons. Tonight she was hampered by all three.

Simple diamond studs—a loan from Rebecca—glittered at her ears. Per Quinn's instructions, she would wear a dress. Per Rebecca's insistence, she would wear high heels. With her hair up in big, fat curlers, she felt like a contestant in a low-end beauty pageant.

"Try this," Rebecca said, handing over another tube.

D.J. cleaned the brush and carefully applied the color. This time her lips looked full and lush. Surprised, she leaned back to judge the effect.

"See?" Rebecca sounded triumphant. "It *can* be perfect. Now dab a little gloss in the center of your bottom lip. It will make you look pouty."

D.J. rolled her eyes. "I'm not the pouty type."

"You are tonight. You're going to knock his socks off."

"I hate to disappoint you but everyone will be keeping his or her clothes on."

Her friend grinned. "So you say now. But that could change. Things happen."

Not likely. Quinn had already turned down sex as payment, and there was no way he would get it any other way. Her interest in the man was strictly business.

"You're too damn cheerful," D.J. muttered as Rebecca began tugging the curlers from her hair.

"I can't help it. You're going on a date with a gorgeous single guy. You're even wearing a dress. I have high hopes that he's the one."

D.J. felt badly for not explaining that the dress had nothing to do with her desire to impress her date, but she wasn't comfortable telling Rebecca about her deal.

"I'm not looking for 'the one,'" she said instead.

"You always say that, but I refuse to believe you. You need the love of a good man."

"Not even on a bet. I'm strong and independent. This two-by-two crap is simply social conditioning."

Rebecca unrolled the last curler, then reached for her brush. "You've missed the point completely," she said as she fluffed curls. "While having someone love you would be nice, the more important lesson is for you to love a man. Cover your eyes."

D.J. didn't want to be having this conversation in the first place, so she dutifully covered her face with her hands and held her breath as her friend doused her in half a can of hair spray. She felt a few picks and tugs, then was completely covered in a second fine, sticky mist.

"Open," Rebecca said.

D.J. peeked through her fingers, then dropped her hands to her lap and groaned. "I look like a porn star."

Rebecca's lips pressed together in disapproval. "We'll get some clothes on you."

D.J. tugged at her robe. "I meant my hair."

"What's wrong with it?"

D.J. gestured with her fingers, but couldn't begin to explain how she felt about the cascading curls tumbling down her back and over her shoulders. Fluffy bangs fell to her eyebrows. She felt all girly and inept.

"You look fabulous," Rebecca said. "Now for the dress."

She disappeared into the closet where D.J. knew the pickings in there were fairly slim. While she would put on a suit for business presentations, that didn't exactly fit the outfit Quinn had described. Most of her dresses were pretty conservative and—

Rebecca reappeared with a box in each hand. The shoe box she'd been expecting, but the other one got her to her feet and glaring.

"No way," she said.

Rebecca dropped the shoe box onto the bed and pulled the top off the other one. "You have to."

"I don't."

Her friend pulled out a black lace dress that D.J. had bought on impulse from a catalog and had never worn.

"It's beautiful."

D.J. shook her head. "It's practically nonexistent."

Rebecca shook out the dress. It was black lace, with a low neckline and a hem that barely covered her thighs. The long sleeves weren't lined, and the back dipped nearly to her fanny. The only thing that kept the shoulders in place was a small section of elastic and prayer.

"Not on a bet," she growled.

"You want to look good for your date, don't you?"

"It's not a date."

"You have to."

"I don't."

"For me?" Rebecca looked beseeching. "Please?"

* * *

The knock came right on time. Quinn crossed to the door and pulled it open. He had a smile prepared, along with a few inconsequential comments. But the sight of D.J. sucked the smart right from his brain.

He opened his mouth, closed it and nearly reached up to rub his eyes. He had to be seeing things. Yeah, he'd demanded a dress, cleavage and leg, but he'd never thought she would listen. He'd expected to be challenged; he hadn't considered he could be blown away.

From the top of her thick, curly hair down to black pumps with a narrow heel sharp enough to be classified as a weapon, she was living, breathing, erotic temptation.

Makeup highlighted her perfect features. The dress—a barely legal scrap of black lace—dipped low enough to expose the space between her breasts and more than hinted at the concealed curves. Long, long, toned legs stretched endlessly, making him wonder what it would be like to have them wrapped around him and pulling him close.

Wanting slammed into him. Wanting and need and more than a little surprise. Damn. She got him good.

But he couldn't risk a compliment. Not when that's what she would be expecting.

"You're on time," he said.

"Whatever. Just so we're all clear. This isn't a date."

"Of course not."

His sports coat hung over the chair by the door. He grabbed it, along with his room key and stepped out into the hall.

"Are we still allowed to have a good time?" he asked as they walked toward the stairs.

"Sure."

He chuckled at the tension in her voice.

When they stepped into the parking lot, she turned toward a black SUV. So the lady wanted them to take her car. Quinn glanced from the high step up to her short dress and couldn't wait to see her climb in.

"Want me to drive?" he asked.

She hesitated, then handed over the keys. "Okay."

He hit the unlock button, then opened her door. She ignored the hand he offered and climbed up into the seat. Her skirt rode up to the top of her thigh, giving him a clear view of female perfection. On cue, heat exploded in his groin, nearly searing him with the intensity.

It was going to be a hell of an evening, he thought as he closed her door and walked around to the driver's side. D.J. taking him prisoner was the best thing to have happened to him in years.

Chapter Six

They were immediately shown to a table in a quiet corner. D.J. was grateful to be out of the line of sight of the front door for a couple of reasons. First, she didn't want to see anyone she knew walking into the restaurant. Second, if she couldn't see the exit, she would be less tempted to bolt for it.

She slid onto the smooth leather of the booth bench and set her small purse next to her. The steak house was dark and elegant, and midweek it was half-empty.

Quinn glanced around. ''Nice place,'' he said. ''Come here often?''

D.J. thought about her nonexistent social life. A big night out for her was joining Rebecca and her family at a pizza place. ''I've been a couple of times. The food is good.''

The waiter appeared and handed them menus,

along with a wine list. As he detailed the specials, Quinn flipped through the wine list.

"May I bring you something to drink?" the waiter asked.

Quinn looked at her. "Do you drink wine?"

"Sure."

He ordered a bottle of cabernet sauvignon.

She'd been thinking more along the lines of half a glass. Not that she would let him know she was concerned, because she wasn't. She would drink as much or as little as she wanted.

When the waiter left, she opened her menu and tried to read the selections. But she was too nervous. Her attention kept snapping back to the man sitting across from her.

He'd been appealing in military garb and tempting in jeans and a shirt. In a suit, he looked like a successful CEO attending a board meeting. The dark fabric of his jacket make his eyes look black. The crisp, white shirt emphasized the firm line of his jaw. His tie looked like silk and was the color of brushed silver.

She shifted slightly and glanced at his face. He was watching her. Thinking what? Did he know he made her nervous? Had he figured out how much she hated that he made her nervous?

Before she could decide, the waiter appeared with the bottle of wine. He opened it expertly, then poured a small amount into Quinn's glass. Quinn rotated the liquid slightly, inhaled the fragrance of the wine, then tasted it.

"Fine," he said with a nod.

After the waiter had poured for both of them and

disappeared, Quinn raised his glass toward her. "To what each of us is about to learn," he said.

She wasn't sure she liked the toast, but she couldn't come up with one on her own. So she touched her glass to his and took a sip of the wine.

It was surprisingly smooth, with lots of flavor, but no bitterness. She was more of a white wine kind of gal, but this wasn't bad.

"Very nice," she said, and set her glass on the table.

"I'm glad you approve." He glanced at her menu. "Do you know what you want?"

She closed her menu and went with what was easy. "Salad, steak, baked potato."

He nodded, then motioned for their waiter. After ordering for her—what was it about the phrase "the lady will have" that sounded so elegant—and himself, he waited until the waiter left, then turned his attention back to her.

"You said you didn't grow up in Glenwood," he told her. "What part of the country are you from?"

D.J. couldn't remember mentioning anything about her past, but maybe she had. They'd chatted during their six-mile run. At least, he'd chatted and she'd panted her way through labored conversation. It was possible she'd gasped out a few insignificant facts while her lungs were screaming for more air.

"I grew up in southern California," she said. "Los Angeles."

"Glenwood must have been an adjustment."

"An easy one."

He raised his dark eyebrows. "Small-town America at its best?"

"Something like that."

She reached for her wine. She didn't want to be talking about herself, she wanted to know about him. What did he do for the government? How long had he trained and where? Was the knife concealed in his collar the only weapon she'd missed in her search of him or had there been others?

All important questions, but she wasn't sure how to make the transition from idle chitchat to real talk. She didn't date much and had never been very good at it. Probably because it had never been important to her.

"I told you that I grew up in a small town in Texas," he said. "Sort of like Glenwood. Everyone knew everyone else. You met my brother, Gage."

She nodded. "Nash and Kevin Harmon, too. All Texas boys."

"More than that." Quinn rested his fingertips on the base of his wineglass. "It's all gotten complicated." He looked up at her and smiled. "Family stuff."

She did her best to ignore the smile and the way her stomach muscles clenched in response. "Complicated how?"

"Nash and Kevin grew up without a father. The guy who got their mom pregnant never wanted anything to do with her or them."

D.J. thought about pointing out that might have been the best for all concerned, but didn't want to distract him from what he was telling her.

"It turns out that their father is the same guy who fathered Gage and me. We're all half brothers to the Hayneses."

D.J. stared in surprise. "I'd heard that old Earl Haynes was something of a ladies' man, but I had no idea his exploits crossed state lines. When did you find this all out?"

"Gage was the first to learn the truth a few months ago. Kevin and Nash found out next. They put a call in to me to meet them here."

She wasn't a fan of having a lot of family, but not everyone was like her. "So you've gone from one brother to more than half a dozen, plus a half sister. That's going to mean sending out a lot more Christmas cards."

He grinned. "I hadn't thought of that."

The waiter appeared with their salads. After he left, Quinn continued.

"You know the Haynes brothers, right?"

"I know Travis and Kyle the best. A lot of my work is coordinated through the sheriff's office. Jordan lives here in town, but he's a fire chief, so we don't have as much contact. I've meet Craig a few times, and Hannah's great."

"They're all in law enforcement," Quinn pointed out. "Except Jordan, and he's close enough."

She picked up her fork and smiled. "They wouldn't agree with you. Everyone gives Jordan a hard time about being a firefighter."

"My brother's a sheriff. Kevin is a U.S. Marshal, Nash works for the FBI and I..." His voice trailed off and he shrugged. "It's strange."

"Not necessarily. A lot of time brothers go into the same line of work. Besides, if you're going to join a ready-made family, this is a good one."

"They're big on wives and kids."

"Actually I think just one wife apiece, but plenty of kids." She took a bite of her salad. "Are you married?"

She thought he might tease her or make a joke, but instead he shook his head. "Not my style."

"Work?"

"That's part of it."

What were the other parts?

"So what does D.J. stand for?" he asked.

"Nothing interesting."

"I don't believe that." He ate some of his salad. When he'd chewed and swallowed he said, "Debbi Jo."

She shook her head.

"Darling Jenny?"

She took another sip of her wine.

"Dashing Joyce?"

"I'm ignoring you."

"Darlene Joy?"

She broke off a piece of bread and bit into it.

"It can't be that bad," he said. "Give me a hint."

D.J. knew it *was* that bad. "I don't hint."

He sighed theatrically. "I'll have to ask around town."

"Ask away. No one knows the truth."

"Really?"

She shrugged. "I keep my secrets."

"What other secrets do you have?"

"If I tell you they won't be secrets."

"Good point." He studied her. "You look beautiful tonight."

The quick shift in topic left her mentally stumbling. Worse, the compliment actually made her toes curl in her too-high and very uncomfortable pumps.

"I, ah, thank you."

"You're welcome. I appreciate that you got into

the spirit of my request for your clothing this evening.''

"I pay my bills in full.''

"Is that what this is?''

"We have a deal. I honored my end, I expect you to do the same.''

He raised his glass as if toasting her again, but he didn't say anything. She watched him drink. There was something about the way he looked at her. He wasn't just watching, he was learning. Studying. The attention should have made her uncomfortable, and in a way it did. But it also left her very aware of his maleness. She'd done the boy-girl thing when it suited her purpose, but never without a reason. Never just because she wanted to.

"You're a hell of a woman, D.J.''

While the quiet praise didn't make her toes curl the same way his telling her she was beautiful had, the sincerity in his voice eased through a tiny crack in her usual solid protective wall. She felt herself relaxing in his presence. Accepting him. Liking him.

The latter should have put her on alert, but she didn't want to think about safety and staying distant. Not for a few more minutes. It felt good to simply *be* in the presence of a man whose company she enjoyed.

"So tell me about growing up in L.A.,'' he said.

Her good mood shattered like a glass dropped on tile. Wariness returned, along with the need to bolt.

"There's not much to tell. I lost my parents when I was eleven. There wasn't any extended family, so I was put into foster care.'' She held up a hand before he could say anything. "The people I was with were fine. Genuinely nice. They worried, they gave a whole lot more than the state paid them to give.''

All true, she thought. In just under seven years she'd been with two different families, and each experience had been textbook perfect. She'd been well fed, clothed, even fussed over on occasion. What no one had figured out was that by the time she was eleven, the damage had already been done.

''I finished high school and went on to college. I had a partial scholarship, some grants and a couple of part-time jobs,'' she continued. ''I graduated and ended up here.''

D.J.'s brief outline of her past was like looking at a black-and-white sketch and being asked to guess the colors that would be used later. There was a broad picture but no detail. Not an accident, Quinn thought. She didn't want anyone to know about her life. He wasn't special in that—he knew she kept the truth from everyone.

He found himself wanting to discover all the nuances that had created the woman sitting across from him. Interesting, as he usually wanted to know only enough to maintain a very temporary relationship. Long weekends were generally the length of his emotional commitment. The less he knew about his women, the less chance he had to find something he didn't like. He leaned toward affairs that touched his body and nothing more.

With D.J. he was willing to risk knowing more. Was it because he sensed she would surprise him only in good ways? He didn't doubt that she would be a hell of a lover—just thinking about all that physical energy and determination channeled into sex was enough to make his breath hitch—but there was another layer that intrigued him. The person underneath the facade. Who was she?

"What about you?" she asked. "How did you get from Possum Landing to Glenwood?"

He pushed away his salad. "After high school, I did the college thing, too."

"Let me guess. You were a football star."

He leaned back in his seat and grinned. "I was very popular."

"I'll bet. A cheerleader on each arm."

"On a good day." He narrowed his gaze. "You would have looked hot in the outfit, but I can't see you being a cheerleader."

"I was too busy winning at my own sports. So did you play in college?"

"Some. After graduation I went into the military. Officer training."

"Of course."

A smile tugged at the corner of her mouth. He responded in kind.

"You're impressed," he said. "It's not the uniform, it's the power."

"Uh-huh. Keep talking."

"Once I had my commission, I was tapped for Special Forces. From there I was moved around."

"Doing things you probably can't talk about."

"Right." He wasn't surprised she understood.

"You said you rescue Americans from places they're not supposed to be. How do they get there?" she asked.

He grimaced. "With enough money, people can persuade a pilot to drop them off just about anywhere. Sometimes what starts out as a safe trip turns bad when there's an unexpected regime change.

Things get hot, and my team and I go in. Most of what I do doesn't get covered in the local press.''

''Of course not.'' She played with her salad fork. ''It must be nice to be away from all that for a few weeks. You don't have to spend all your time looking over your shoulder.''

He nodded.

In the subtle lighting there were hints of red in her dark-brown hair. The loose curls brushed across her shoulders and down her chest, drawing his gaze to the cleavage exposed by her low-cut dress. Despite the lace covering her arms, he could still see the definition of her muscles.

She wasn't like anyone he'd ever met.

''Don't you want to ask if I've ever killed anyone?'' he asked, because it was a question his dates eventually got around to.

He should have known better.

D.J. picked up her wine. ''It wouldn't occur to me that you haven't. You wouldn't get your kind of experience any other way. You are who and what you are for a reason.''

The quiet acceptance in her voice tempted him. There had been a time when he'd thought normal might be possible. That he could find the one woman who would understand. Who could accept what he did and know why. He'd long ago given up on the hope of finding her. There was no way she existed…or did she? Was D.J. a possibility or was he fantasizing, based on a tough talk and perfect thighs?

''You did promise that you'd be in town for a few weeks,'' she said as the waiter cleared their plates. "I expect a return on my investment." She plucked at her long sleeve as she spoke.

"I'm on indefinite leave."

She waited until the waiter left before leaning forward. "Why? Were you injured?"

Not in the way she meant. "I want to consider my options. My work requires a level of disconnection I need to be willing to continue. Maybe it's time for a change."

This was the first time he'd verbalized what he'd been thinking about for the past few weeks. He waited to see if the words felt right or not. When there was no definitive answer, he finished his wine and reached for the bottle.

"I was supposed to kill someone and couldn't." He poured himself another glass and topped up hers. "I'd never refused an assignment before. Never had reason. But this time…" Everything had been different, he thought grimly.

Her dark gaze never left his face. There was no recoil, no disgust, no foolish questions.

"You had a good reason for refusing," she said. She wasn't asking, she was announcing.

"Yeah."

There was no way she could know, but he liked her assumption. She was right.

He'd been sent to kill a double agent. It had happened before and he didn't mind killing one of his own if the operative had crossed to the other side. But the double agent had turned out to be someone Quinn had known for years. His former commanding officer and mentor. He'd felt as if he'd been trapped in a bad spy movie, only the players and the bullets were real. When the time came, he couldn't do it. He'd had the man in his sights and he'd been unable to pull the trigger.

Someone else had been sent in to take care of the problem, and he'd been brought out for evaluation. When he'd asked for leave, it had been granted. Until then he hadn't minded what he did for a living, but he knew he couldn't keep cleaning up messes like that—not without paying with the price of his soul.

Silence surrounded them. Quinn searched for a casual topic, some distraction. He didn't usually talk about his work in any detail. He certainly never told the truth. So why had he with D.J.?

She tilted her head. "So when you sneak into foreign countries, you probably don't get the exotic stamps on your passport, huh?"

"No. Under those circumstances we tend to avoid immigration."

"Bummer. The stamps are the best part of traveling."

Her easy acceptance relaxed him as much as it made him curious. "Why aren't you involved with someone?"

"I'm not an idiot. I don't need a testosterone-filled male dominating my life. What's in it for me? More work? More financial obligations? I don't think so."

Her answer made him chuckle. "What about kids?"

She smiled. "I would like children." She made a show of glancing around the restaurant, then she leaned close. "What with you being out of the country and all, you may not have heard. Marriage isn't required for children anymore."

"You're kidding?"

"Nope. Isn't modern science amazing?"

The waiter arrived with their entrees. As they were served, Quinn watched D.J. There was a reason she was so against marriage in general and men in particular. Someone, somewhere had hurt her. Who had done it and how? He knew there was no way she would tell him, but that didn't stop him from wanting to know.

When they arrived in the parking lot of his hotel, D.J. gave Quinn a pointed look. He knew she expected him to say good-night and climb right out of her car, but he didn't plan to make things that easy for her.

"Why don't you pull into a parking space for a few minutes?" he asked.

She sighed heavily, as if this was a major inconvenience, then steered the SUV into a parking place and turned off the engine.

He was amused by her insistence at driving back from the restaurant. She'd said it would be so much easier to just drop him off. The implication being that she wasn't about to go up to his room. Just as well, he hadn't planned on asking her. Not yet.

"What time do you want to start tomorrow?" he asked.

"Mornings are best for me."

"That's fine. Your place had all the equipment we'll need. You did a good job outfitting it."

"Thanks. It's part of my work. I hold weekly classes there for women."

"Not men?"

She shrugged. "They're welcome to attend, but

they never do. Guys don't have the same issues. While there are some unprovoked attacks in the animal world, humans are the only species where the females instinctively fear unfamiliar males. No man walking down a dark street at night thinks anything about seeing a lone woman, but that same woman is aware of every man around her."

He'd never thought of it in those terms. "I guess you're right," he said.

The lights in the parking lot illuminated her face enough for him to see her roll her eyes.

"Gee, thanks."

He held in a grin. "You don't strike me as the type of woman who is often afraid."

"I'm not, but I take care of myself. I know how to fight and when to get out of the way. I don't put myself into dangerous situations."

He leaned toward her. "I'm dangerous."

"You're a known danger, and I'm prepared."

"Not possible."

"Want to bet?"

She was bluffing. They both knew that he could take her easily. Yet she faced him fearlessly.

"Tough as nails," he murmured. "It's one of the things I like best about you."

Her eyes widened and her mouth parted. She looked stunned by his statement. Stunned and maybe a little pleased? He couldn't tell.

Tension flared between them, and he took it as a good sign. Awareness was only one step removed from arousal, and he sure wanted her plenty aroused.

He braced one hand on the dashboard and leaned toward her. But before he'd moved more than a couple of inches, she stiffened. The reaction was subtle, something he felt rather than saw. He stilled instantly, then relaxed back into his seat.

Another man might have been discouraged or figured she wasn't worth the effort. Quinn knew better. There was something to be said for a woman who was—to quote Shakespeare—''not so quickly won.''

He rubbed his eyes. Shakespeare? He was quoting Shakespeare? Damn, but he had it bad.

''We're going to have to figure out how many lessons dinner was worth,'' he said casually.

She turned her head to glare at him. ''A dinner I paid for,'' she snapped.

He stared out the front window and faked a yawn. ''I offered. You insisted.'' He'd backed off because an instinct had told him that was the better strategy. ''The dress was great. And those shoes—pure fantasy material.''

''Five lessons,'' she told him.

''Two.''

''Three.''

''Deal.''

He put his right arm on the door by the window and rested his left on the console between their seats. ''Okay. You can kiss me now, but I want you to really put some effort into it. It needs to be better than that last kiss.''

If D.J. had had a weapon at her disposal, she would have killed him. Right there in her vehicle, knowing it was going to mess up her leather seats. Fury roared through her. She wanted to scream, to kick, to grind his bones into dust, then bake them into bread and leave it out for the crows.

How dare he? *She* could kiss *him?* The nerve. The

absolute, unadulterated nerve of his pompous, egotistical, self-centered—

"I can hear you sputtering," Quinn said mildly,
his eyes half-closed. He turned toward her.
"Afraid?"

He nailed her with that one word. Damn him, he'd
probably known it would work. She found it amazingly difficult not to rise to a challenge.

She clamped down on the knee-jerk response and
forced herself to smile casually. "Not interested."

"Of course you are. Just come get what you want,
D.J. I'm all yours."

She wanted to slap him. Worse, she wanted to do
what he said and kiss him. She *hated* that he was
right—that she *was* interested. Why did he get to
her? She didn't want to be interested. Not in him.
She hated that her stomach got all tight and her toes
curled and, yes, that more than once during dinner
she'd thought about them kissing and, well, maybe
doing more.

It was crazy. She knew the danger of getting involved. Of caring and being vulnerable. She simply
didn't let it happen. Not ever.

There was only one solution, she told herself. She
had to bring Quinn to his knees and not get involved
herself. That would teach him to mess with her.

She drew in a deep breath, then slid closer. The
console was between them, so she had to lean over
to reach his mouth. She braced herself for the embrace that was sure to follow. His arms would close
around her and she would want to bolt. But he didn't
try to hold her at all. Instead his hands stayed where
they were and she was free to stretch until her mouth
touched his.

The second they kissed she was assaulted on several levels. The heat of him. The firm softness of his lips. The scent of his body and how the male fragrance teased at her. Awareness melted through her, making her muscles relax and her thighs clench. Wanting, she thought, both aroused and dismayed. She wanted him.

Fear battled with the need to prove herself, and his challenge won. She brushed her lips against his, discovering the shape, the edges, before tilting her head slightly and parting her mouth.

He accepted her invitation with a quick stroke of his tongue against her bottom lip. Tiny jolts of need zapped through her body. She had to shift her weight so she could get closer, all the while ignoring the sudden sensitivity of her breasts.

When his tongue slipped inside her mouth, she touched it with her own. The heat surprised her, as did the sweet taste and growing need. She was melting. Disappearing into the passion. Against her will, one of her hands crept up to settle on his chest. She could feel the warmth of him, even through his suit jacket. She wanted him to take it off, that and his shirt. She wanted to feel bare skin. To feel *him.*

Even as her body surrendered, her mind went on alert. She told herself this was not a good idea. That men were inherently dangerous, and none more so than Quinn. The hunger had to be controlled. Sex was a weapon, not something she could risk enjoying. Not ever.

Her throat felt tight. She swallowed against sudden dryness. Funny that her throat was so dry when other parts of her were so very wet.

One of Quinn's hands settled lightly on her back.

She braced herself against the need to escape, only
it never came. She didn't want to run away; she
wasn't afraid. She was hungry. Starving. She wanted
him to touch her more. Everywhere. She wanted to
be naked, with him inside of her. She wanted his
hands on her body. She wanted to hear the screams
of her own surrender.

The image of them making love filled her brain.
It was so real, so vivid, that she half expected to
feel the thrust of his penetration. It was so immediate that fear swamped her. She straightened in her
seat and tried to keep him from seeing that she was
shaking.

"It's late," she said abruptly. She stared straight
ahead, not wanting to look at his face and know
what he was thinking.

There were several heartbeats of silence. "I'll see
you about nine in the morning," he said.

She was afraid if she spoke anymore her voice
would crack, so she only nodded. He opened the car
door and climbed out.

After changing into sweats, D.J. paced the length
of her cottage house. Usually the small rooms were
a sanctuary, but tonight the space was cramped and
confining. She felt restless and knew the cause.

Quinn.

Hunger burned in her. Hunger and wanting and
need and all those dark emotions she avoided. Now
she knew why. They kept her body from being a
tool. They made her edgy, vulnerable.

Why had she kissed him? She shook her head.
Silly question. She'd kissed him because she'd
wanted to, and now she paid the price. He'd aroused

her, but more than that, he'd touched something inside. He made her weak, and she knew what that meant. Weakness meant danger was close. Very close. The strong crushed the weak. Broke them into pieces and left them for dead.

Chapter Seven

Quinn stepped into the small diner at seven the next morning. Travis had left a message at his hotel, inviting Quinn to join him for breakfast.

He saw the other man at a booth by the front window and nodded at the hostess as he made his way back.

"Morning," he said as he approached.

Travis set down the paper he'd been reading and poured coffee from a carafe left on the table. "How's it going? I wasn't sure you'd want to get up this early."

Quinn shrugged. "I don't sleep much."

A job hazard, he thought. Years of not being able to relax meant that sleep was hard to come by. Last night he'd added sexual frustration to his list of reasons he couldn't doze off. Kissing D.J. had left him hard and more than ready to have his way with her.

Talk about a hell of a kiss. Still, it had been worth every sleepless toss and turn.

Travis glanced at his watch. "My brothers and Hannah have an open invitation to join me, but they know if they're not here by five after seven, I go ahead and order without them. I guess it's just you and me this morning."

Quinn drank some of the black, steamy coffee and leaned back in the booth. "Not a problem. How's the sheriff business?"

"We're having a quiet summer, which is good. In another month the high school kids will start to get restless. They'll get involved in petty stuff." His dark gaze settled on Quinn. "Nothing like what you're used to."

Quinn shrugged. He knew that Gage would have mentioned what he did, but only in the most general terms. "Small towns have their advantages. You don't have to watch your back so much."

"Good point." Travis smiled. "So how was dinner?"

Quinn wasn't surprised that news traveled fast, although he doubted D.J. would be amused to know they'd been the subject of gossip.

"Good. The company was better."

"I was surprised to hear you and D.J. were going out."

"Because she doesn't date much?"

Travis hesitated. "She's a private person."

Nice save, Quinn thought. He appreciated that Travis was trying to protect someone he cared about, and he liked that D.J. wasn't as alone as she pretended.

"She's a complex woman," Quinn said.

"Aren't they all?"

"I don't claim to understand them," Quinn admitted. D.J. less than most. There was something in her past that had her on the run. Not physically, but emotionally. While she'd easily offered him sex in exchange for him teaching her what he knew, last night she'd completely panicked in the middle of a kiss. He had enough ego to want to believe she'd been blown away by his great technique, but he had to admit there was more on the line than that. Something had scared her, and he wanted to know what.

"What's going on between the two of you?" Travis asked bluntly.

"She's hired me to teach her a few moves."

"I have an idea about what you do, more from what your brother didn't say than what he did," Travis told him. "You beat D.J. at the games, which no one has done before, so I understand why she would want to learn from you. But that doesn't explain dinner."

Quinn wasn't sure he was willing to admit that D.J. having dinner with him had been his payment for three lessons.

"She's a beautiful woman," Quinn said by way of stalling.

"Most guys can't get past how tough she is to notice."

"*I* noticed."

Travis smiled. "I want to ask what you plan to do about it and I don't have the right."

"Don't sweat it. I like knowing D.J. has someone looking out for her."

"Yeah? Don't tell her about it. She'll bite my head off."

"After she breaks your legs," Quinn agreed with a grin.

"Am I too late?"

Quinn turned toward the speaker, a tall man with long, dark hair and an earring. Travis moved over to make room.

"Austin. You're up early."

The other man nodded and slid into the booth. When he was settled, he stretched his hand across the table.

"Austin Lucas."

"Quinn Reynolds."

They shook hands.

Quinn took in the too-long hair, the cool, gray eyes and the sharp, intelligent gaze. He recognized the signs of another loner.

"Austin is an honorary Haynes," Travis said, handing his friend his menu. "We've been hanging out since we were kids."

"I've met your brother, Gage," Austin said. "He's a good man."

"I agree."

The waitress appeared then and took their orders. She replaced the empty carafe with a full one, brought another mug for Austin, then left them alone.

"We were talking about D.J.," Travis said. "Quinn had dinner with her last night."

"I'm surprised," Austin said. "Normally she likes to chew men up and spit them out before breakfast."

His knowledge implied a level of intimacy that made Quinn uneasy. He tried to define the tightness he felt inside. Annoyance? Jealousy?

He studied the man across from him, and Austin met his gaze. Apparently Austin read the concern there because he said, "D.J. is good friends with my wife. They couldn't be more different, but Rebecca says that's what makes the relationship interesting."

"D.J.'s an interesting woman," Quinn said.

Austin glanced at Travis. "Should we be worried?"

"Not about me. I'm one of the good guys," Quinn said.

"Are you?" Austin sounded surprised.

Quinn supposed it was a fair question. There were almost no circumstances under which he would describe himself that way. Except for this one. He had agreed to give D.J. what she wanted, and he would. In the process he was unlikely to damage her heart.

Travis leaned forward. "Quinn, you're family now, and we all look out for each other. The thing is, we look out for D.J., too. I guess we're going to have to trust you to respect that. Fair enough?"

"Sure."

Quinn agreed easily, but he had a bad feeling that life had just taken a turn for the complicated.

By morning D.J. had herself under control. She'd put the kiss and her reaction to it in perspective and decided she would forget it ever happened. Yes, she'd reacted to the man, but so what? Her life had very specific priorities, and being the best was the primary one. Quinn had information she wanted and she was going to get it. End of story.

As for payment for future lessons, they would have to negotiate that when the time came. She was opposed to any more dates. They were—

The front door to her office opened, and the man in question strolled in. Whatever she'd been thinking flew from her mind, like a flock of sparrows frightened by a stalking cat.

But the mental hiccup wasn't nearly as annoying as her visceral reaction to his large, male presence. The second he walked in, her mouth went dry, her palms went wet and her thighs caught fire. It was damned annoying.

"Morning," he said cheerfully, as he shut the door behind him. "You know what they say—'When the student is ready, the teacher will appear.' Here I am. You'd better be ready."

She tried to smile at his humor, but she was too caught up in how tall and broad he looked. The shorts he wore emphasized his long, powerful legs. His T-shirt stretched over muscles that could probably bench-press the weight of half a cheerleading squad.

"Did you sleep well?" he asked.

"Of course," she said, lying through her teeth.

He looked calm and rested, as if he hadn't been bothered by their kiss. Fine. If he could play that game, so could she. Better than him in fact.

He crossed to stand next to her, then put his hand on her shoulder. "Let's go."

"Fine by me."

As she turned toward the back, she casually shrugged off his touch and raced into the workout room. She hated the heat that lingered on her skin and the heaviness she felt low in her belly. The irony of the situation was that she was far more worried about her sexual reaction to him than by his potential to physically hurt her. Most women, if they knew the truth about what he did, would have been terrified to simply be in the same room with him. D.J. could trust his professionalism while they worked out. It was his guyness and sensual appeal that made her sweat.

Once in the back, they went through a series of warm-up exercises and stretches. Like Quinn, D.J. wore shorts and a T-shirt. She'd pulled her hair back in a French braid. She wanted to be free to move, but she didn't look forward to a lot of skin-on-skin contact. Telling herself she wouldn't react was one thing. Remembering what had happened the previous night and knowing the potential for sexual disaster was another.

Before they walked to the mats, they both tugged off their shoes and socks.

"We'll take this slow," Quinn said as he moved into the center of the mat. "You remember what we did last time?"

She nodded. They'd been working on a frontal assault.

"I showed you how to counteract it," he said.

"You showed me, but it didn't work."

He grinned. "I'm really good."

"Quit bragging. This session isn't about you."

"Fair enough. So let's go."

He faced her and waited for the attack. She moved in and mentally braced herself for his response. Seconds later she landed flat on her back.

"I remember this part," she grumbled as she scrambled to her feet.

"We'll take it slow," he told her. "Watch me."

Forty minutes later she was making progress. She could count on a draw about 20 percent of the time and victory about 30 percent of the time. Which meant the other 50 percent of the attacks could leave her dead.

"This is why you get the big bucks," she said as she once again sailed through the air and landed on the mats, staring at the ceiling.

"You know it."

He stuck out his hand to pull her to her feet. The movement was familiar enough that she barely hesitated before taking the offered help. When she was standing, she wiped the sweat from her forehead. Quinn, of course, still looked morning-shower fresh.

"I'm going to come at you from behind," he said, moving in close. "There are several traditional attack positions."

His body pressed against hers and his arm came around her throat. Her attention split neatly down the middle. One half reveled in his heat and the large hand resting on her waist. Even as her bones began to turn to liquid, the rest of her fought against a powerful fight-or-flight response.

"You can easily get away from this hold," Quinn said. "Keep your chin down and go for leverage. A more controlled and deadly attack will put pressure here."

He shifted until his hand cupped her throat. Instantly her fear escalated until she desperately wanted to break free and run. The second he pressed in with his thumb, her stomach rolled and adrenaline flooded her system.

"The difference between stopping blood to the brain long enough to knock someone out or kill them is all a matter of degree," he said, sounding amazingly conversational.

She drew back her arm to elbow him in the mid-section. From there she would grab his arm and pull him over her—

He released her and stepped away. "Now you try it on me."

The panic faded as quickly as it had appeared. There was only the chemical aftermath that left her feeling shaky and slightly light-headed.

Ignoring the sensations, she stepped behind him and raised herself on tiptoe so she could wrap an arm around his throat.

"We have a height problem," she muttered as her breasts flattened against his back. "This would be easier if you were shorter."

"Hey, nothing worth having is easy."

"Thanks for the bumper-sticker-level psycho-babble."

She tried to squeeze his neck with her hand, but she couldn't get a good grip. The warmth of his skin and the scent of his body didn't help her concentration, nor did the fact that her hands were small. She felt inconsequential and feminine. Neither reality thrilled her.

"Can't I just shoot you?" she asked.

"It would shorten our lesson time," he said, and bent his knees. "Is this better?"

She was able to grip more firmly. "It helps."

"Don't get used to it. Once you've mastered the technique, you'll have to deal with me at my full height. You can't always be sure your assailants will be shorter than you."

She was about to agree with his point when she heard a familiar voice calling out her name. A quick glance at the clock showed her it was nearly ten-thirty. Time had flown.

"Back here," she called, and stepped away from Quinn. "I guess we'll take our break now."

He turned toward the doorway and raised his eyebrows when Rebecca entered. D.J. followed his gaze and nearly groaned.

Just perfect, she thought, heading for the small refrigerator and pulling out a bottle of water. She was hot, sweaty and badly dressed. Rebecca was feminine perfection in a white summer dress, perfect makeup and tasteful pearl earrings. Tiny flat sandals exposed the pink polish on her toes. D.J. had never been jealous of her friend before and refused to start now. What did she care if Quinn thought Rebecca was the perfect woman? Not only *wasn't* she interested in him, her friend was happily married and hadn't looked at another man since meeting Austin nearly ten years ago.

So why did D.J. suddenly feel like a "before" picture in a magazine makeover?

"You have company," Rebecca said. She had a carafe in one hand and a box of Krispy Kremes in the other. "Am I interrupting?"

"Not at all." D.J. jerked her head at Quinn without actually looking at him. She didn't want to see him drooling. "Rebecca, this is Quinn. He's teaching me to be a better fighter."

"That statement begs a thousand questions," Rebecca said as she set the doughnuts on a table and put the coffee next to them. Then she crossed to the mats and held out her hand. "Nice to meet you, Quinn."

"Likewise."

Despite her best intention, D.J. glanced at the two of them. They seemed to be caught up in a staring contest...and still clasping hands, she thought glumly. Not that she cared. Men like him didn't interest her. No men interested her. She didn't do the romantic, boy-girl thing. Remember?

"I met your husband this morning when I joined Travis Haynes for breakfast."

Rebecca pulled her hand free and sighed. "Isn't he wonderful?"

D.J. took comfort in the fact that if Quinn had been blown away by Rebecca's feminine charms, he'd just received a dose of reality. She might be pretty enough to have her portrait in the National Gallery, but she was a one-man woman. And Austin was her man.

"'Wonderful' isn't how guys describe each other," Quinn told her.

Rebecca smiled. "Good point. Would you be willing to describe D.J. that way?"

He turned his gaze on her. D.J. drank from her water bottle and tried not to care. "Maybe."

"I think that's secretly a yes." Rebecca linked arms with him. "I stop by in the morning a couple of times a week. I bring fattening food and coffee. D.J. and I do girl talk and get a sugar high. Harmless fun, but we like it."

They walked out of the workout room, leaving D.J. to grab the doughnuts and coffee and trail after them.

"What do you do?" Quinn asked.

"Mostly I'm a wife and mother, but I work part-time at the Glenwood Orphanage. I used to run it, but after I married Austin and started having babies, there wasn't time.''

"You're very traditional.''

"I suppose so.''

When D.J. reached her office, Rebecca and Quinn had already pulled up chairs around her desk. She sank into her seat and slapped the doughnut box in front of them, not sure why she was irritated. So Rebecca was talking to Quinn. What did that matter? Wasn't it easier than D.J. having to talk to him?

Rebecca winked at her, then turned her attention back to Quinn. "Don't let the modest offices fool you. Our D.J. is very successful. She flies all over the country, sometimes all over the world, rescuing children. She gives lectures and demonstrations.''

D.J. grabbed a doughnut. "I'm still in the room you know.''

Rebecca smiled. "Of course you're here, but I doubt you've been talking about all your accomplishments.'' She glanced back at Quinn. "D.J. can be very modest.''

D.J. bit into the doughnut and rolled her eyes.

Quinn reached into the box. "She mentioned that she helps when kids are abducted.''

"Yes. There's a lot of danger, but she goes right in. She looks tough, but the kids are never scared of her. I guess they sense she only wants to help.''

This was as painful as dental surgery, D.J. thought. She didn't like being talked about.

"Let's change the subject,'' she said brightly. "Let's talk about Quinn. Guys like to be the center of attention.''

Rebecca looked surprised. "I didn't know you

knew that." She turned to Quinn. "Where are you from?"

"A small town in Texas."

"I know you have a brother. Well, I suppose now you have several. What about your mom? Are you close to her?"

D.J. frowned. Talk about a strange question. Rebecca turned to her. "Don't give me that look. How a man treats his mother can be an indication of character. Well, unless she's a horrible woman, like Austin's mother was."

Quinn grinned. "My mom is terrific and I get along with her extremely well."

D.J. wanted to crawl under the table. Great. So Rebecca wasn't even going to be subtle about the matchmaking.

"Are you seeing anyone?" her friend asked.

The second the question was out, D.J. wanted to smack her head into the desk. Was Quinn seeing anyone? Had she even thought to ask that herself? The man could be married, and she'd been offering him sex.

She held her breath until he said he wasn't involved at this time.

"Have you ever been married?" Rebecca asked.

Quinn glanced at D.J. "You could rescue me here."

"Why?"

He laughed. "No," he told Rebecca. "No ex-wives."

"What about significant relationships?"

"My work keeps me on the move."

"Uh-huh." Rebecca delicately bit into a doughnut, chewed and swallowed. "That's a better excuse than some people have.'' She stared intently at D.J., then smiled at Quinn. ''D.J. doesn't get out much, which you may have noticed. Not that she doesn't need to.''

D.J. glared at her. ''I'm still right here in the room.''

''We all know that. I'm just stating the obvious.''

''So what exactly is her dating history?'' Quinn asked.

''It's very sad,'' Rebecca told him. ''It's not that men aren't interested. A lot of them are. Some of the problem is her surly attitude.''

D.J. had just bitten into a doughnut and found herself choking. Rebecca pounded her on the back until she waved the other woman off.

''My surly attitude?'' she asked, outraged.

Rebecca merely smiled. ''Am I wrong? Do you in any way encourage men to be a part of your life? Don't you make a habit of scaring off anyone even faintly interested?''

''Okay, then,'' D.J. said as she stood. ''You probably need to get going.''

Quinn leaned back in his chair and grinned. ''Don't make her rush off on my account.''

''Of course not,'' D.J. said, trying to ignore him and her rising embarrassment. ''You would love to sit here and listen to wild stories about my past.''

''It's more interesting than cable TV.''

Rebecca rose. ''I'm trying to help,'' she said as she collected her purse. ''Quinn seems very nice.''

D.J. wanted to die. She couldn't believe that her friend—make that her *ex*-friend—was acting this way.

"I'm not going to be speaking to you later," D.J. told her.

Rebecca patted her arm. "Of course you are." She walked to the front door, then turned back. "It was nice to meet you, Quinn. Don't let her scare you off."

"Likewise," Quinn said. "Your husband's a lucky man."

Rebecca sighed. "He knows. Oh! There's going to be a big dinner at my house tomorrow night. Just another Haynes get-together for the new members of the family to commingle with the rest. I hope you'll be there."

"I wouldn't miss it."

Rebecca turned her attention to D.J. "I'm really going to need your help setting up things."

"Not even on a bet."

"D.J., you have to."

Rebecca wasn't being subtle, but D.J. figured arguing in front of Quinn would only increase his entertainment factor. She gritted her teeth and nodded.

"Fine. I'll be there."

"Good."

Rebecca wiggled her fingers at them both and ducked out of the room. D.J. stared after her and thought briefly about throwing a chair across the room, but wasn't sure it would do anything for her frustration level. At least she had plenty of energy to continue sparring with Quinn.

"Let's get back to work," she told him as she rose and headed for the back of the office.

He didn't budge. "Not so fast. I have a question."

D.J. could only imagine. "How did Rebecca and I get to be friends?"

"Nope. What do the initials stand for?"

She blinked at him. He wanted to know her real name? "Not even on a bet."

"I'm not going to help you until you tell me."

She narrowed her gaze. "I've already paid for my lessons. You owe me."

"Maybe, but I'm not moving until you cough up the truth."

She stared at him. He looked comfortable and more than prepared to sit there well into the afternoon. She considered her options: there weren't any. She couldn't force him to move and she couldn't continue the lessons without him.

She sucked in a breath and braced herself for the laughter. "Daisy Jane."

Quinn's mouth twitched, but that was his only reaction. "It suits you," he said.

She took a step toward him. "Don't make me kill you."

His twitch turned into a grin. "You couldn't even bruise me, little girl. Let's go."

Chapter Eight

Quinn arrived at the party shortly after seven. Judging by the number of cars in the driveway, there was a houseful of guests. After parking his rental car, he sat in the driver's seat for a few seconds and told himself this was just a family event. No danger, no threats.

The reminder wasn't to make himself feel better, but to keep himself from going into work mode. Crowds usually put him on alert. He'd had to rescue more than one hostage from an overflowing temporary prison or a bustling outdoor marketplace. He knew how to move without being seen, how to slip in and out with no one realizing he'd ever been there at all. Not exactly qualities that would make him a favorite guest.

He climbed out of the car and pocketed the keys,

then headed for the front door. It opened before he could knock.

Rebecca Lucas stood in the foyer and smiled at him. "Right on time."

He jerked his head toward the crowd behind her. "Was everyone else early?"

She laughed. "The women and kids started arriving around four. The husbands are just starting to follow. As for this being 'everyone else,' you haven't seen all your extended family in one place yet, have you?"

He shook his head.

She smiled. "Then brace yourself."

She took his arm and drew him inside her large, welcoming home. He had a brief impression of warm colors, oversize furniture and lots of people.

"Most of the kids are out back playing," Rebecca said. "But a few of them are running around. I won't even try to match them with parents just now. You'll be doing well if you can remember who is married to whom."

She paused by three women and introduced them as Elizabeth, Travis's wife, Jill, Craig's wife and Holly, Jordan's wife.

Quinn nodded and shook hands. He had a good memory for faces and names, but keeping this group straight was going to be a challenge.

"Hannah's around here somewhere," Rebecca told him. "She's an actual Haynes. Her mother is over there. Louise knew Earl back when she was in high school. There's still Sandy, who isn't here yet. You know all the Texas clan, as we're calling them. Oh, there's Gage."

Quinn turned and saw his brother walking toward

him. Gage smiled at Rebecca. "Quinn's getting that trapped look, so I'm going to rescue him before he bolts."

Rebecca nodded. "We are overwhelming all at once. I had the advantage of meeting the brothers individually. When I married Austin, only Travis had a wife. So I've been able to get to know everyone slowly. You're being thrown into the deep end. Let me know if you need a life preserver."

"Will do."

She patted his arm and walked off.

Gage led him to the kitchen where a cooler filled with beer and sodas sat on the counter.

"How you doing?" his brother asked.

"Fine."

"Too much family?"

Quinn considered the question. He'd never been much of a joiner, and he rarely hung out with friends. But that was more about circumstance than temperament.

"I'm okay as long as there's not a quiz on names."

Gage chuckled. "We've all been through that one. You'll figure it out."

While Gage pulled out two beers and opened them, Quinn glanced around at the kitchen and family room. Several kids gathered around the coffee table and played a board game. Nash and Kevin sat on the sofa. Stephanie stood next to Nash, her hand on his shoulder, his arm around her waist.

He turned in the opposite direction, back the way he'd come. There were the wives he'd met, a few kids and...

Damn, he thought silently and shook his head. He

wasn't just checking out the surroundings; he was looking for D.J.

She was prickly, difficult and spent most of their time together wanting to bash his head in. So why was he so hot to see her again? He accepted the beer his brother offered, and grinned. Because she was never boring.

He spotted movement by the back door and glanced toward it. D.J. stepped into the house. She wore a short-sleeved shirt tucked into jeans. Instead of her usual boots, she had on open-toed sandals. Her hair was loose, her expression happy. She had a little girl by the hand and bent down to hear what she said. After listening intently, D.J. nodded, then pointed toward the front of the house. The little girl—tiny, with pigtails and a bright-pink shorts set—released D.J. and ran in the direction she'd pointed. D.J. straightened.

He knew the exact second she caught sight of him. Not only did their gazes lock, but the temperature in the room climbed about forty degrees.

Gage handed him a beer. "Isn't that the woman from the war games?" he asked when he saw her.

"Yeah. D.J."

"Short for?"

Quinn shrugged. No way was he going tell the world her secret. Calling her Daisy Jane would be something he did in private.

Kari walked into the kitchen, and Quinn greeted his brother's fiancée.

"How was San Francisco?" he asked.

Kari leaned against Gage and smiled. "Good. How are you, Quinn? I haven't seen you in forever."

"I'm well. Congratulations on your engagement." He waved his beer bottle toward his brother. "You know Gage is getting the good end of the deal, don't you?"

Tall and pretty, with big blue eyes and an easy smile, Kari had always been a small-town beauty. Gage had been crazy about her from the second they'd met. But once she'd left Possum Landing, Quinn had figured they were through for good. Funny how they'd finally hooked up again.

Kari rested her head on Gage's shoulder. "I think we're both getting a good deal."

"All that and a diplomat," Quinn said. "How'd you get so lucky?"

Gage shrugged. "The results of living right."

"Dumb luck if you ask me."

Kari eyed him. "You could find someone, Quinn."

"Not likely," he told her, then took a long drink of his beer.

"My brother's lifestyle doesn't allow for anything longer than a fifteen-minute relationship," Gage said.

"Lifestyles change."

Kari had a point. Quinn excused himself and turned. D.J. wasn't by the back door any longer, but he knew she hadn't left the house. He headed for the living room and found her talking with Rebecca.

"Ladies," he said as he approached.

Rebecca winked at D.J. "It's your young man."

D.J. groaned. "He's not my anything."

"He's something, because I can feel the heat between you two from here."

"What you're feeling is a premature hot flash."

Rebecca laughed. "Not even close." She looked at Quinn. "Maybe you should consider getting her drunk."

D.J.'s eyes widened. "Rebecca, you can't be serious. That's a horrible thing to say."

"Quinn isn't going to hurt you, and you need to lighten up. And I need to take care of my other guests."

She smiled at them both, then sauntered away. D.J. narrowed her eyes and watched her go.

"I can't believe she would sell me out like that. Statistically women who get drunk while—"

"Shut up, Daisy Jane."

Her mouth dropped open. "What did you say?"

"You heard me. Whatever the statistics may be, they don't apply to this situation and you know it. Quit acting like I'm some college kid out to take whatever he can regardless of the consequences."

Several emotions flashed across her face. If they had been alone, he was pretty sure she would have exploded into some kind of fit, but the presence of the extended Haynes family would keep her quiet.

"Don't call me that name," she whispered through gritted teeth.

"Why not?"

"I hate it."

"It's charming."

She looked mad enough to spit. Instead she crossed her arms and contented herself with glaring. "I can't believe I'm stuck here," she grumbled. "Rebecca lied about needing help. When I arrived, there wasn't one thing for me to do, so this was all a ploy."

"Sure. She's trying to get us together."

"Doesn't that bother you?"

"Nope. It shouldn't bother you, either. Rebecca cares about you."

D.J. grunted in response. "She needs a hobby."

"I think you're it."

Three kids about ten or eleven burst into the house and ran toward the kitchen. D.J. stepped out of the way.

"There's a pool table in back," she said. "Want to see if it's available?"

"Sure."

As she turned to lead the way, he put his hand on the small of her back. She froze and looked at him.

"What do you think you're doing?"

"Being polite," he said.

She'd gotten all stiff. He could feel her muscles practically locking in place. Despite her obvious displeasure, tension crackled between them.

"I can get from point A to point B without assistance," she said and pushed his hand away.

"Why are you so afraid?" he asked, his voice low.

"I'm not. Just because I don't like to be mauled, doesn't mean there's anything wrong with me."

"A good story but I'm not buying."

"Fine. Because I wasn't selling."

They wove through the crowd. Quinn couldn't keep from grinning. D.J. sure as hell wouldn't make it easy, but when he finally won her, it was going to be worth all the effort. He had a feeling he'd never met anyone like her before and was unlikely to do so in the future.

He supposed there were men who would see D.J.

as a woman to be tamed, but not him. He liked her feisty and difficult. He wanted her strong enough to stand up for herself and comfortable telling him to go to hell if that was where she thought he should be.

The game room was huge, with a pool table in the center, and three full-size video games set up along the far wall. A big fireplace stood in a corner. They had the space to themselves.

D.J. pulled the cover off the table and folded it. Quinn pulled balls out of pockets and set them on the table.

"I haven't played in a while," he said. "I'd like to take some practice shots."

"No problem." She leaned against the table and smiled. "What are we playing for?"

"Is everything a competition with you?"

"Pretty much."

"What if two people happen to have a mutual goal?" he asked.

She shrugged. "How often does that happen in life?"

"What about at work?"

"Okay. There, but almost nowhere else."

"I can think of a couple of places."

She sighed heavily. "Is everything about sex with you?"

He grinned. "Pretty much."

The corner of her mouth twitched and he knew she'd recognized her own words tossed back at her.

"We could play for money," she said.

"Not interesting enough. What about articles of clothing?"

D.J. shook her head. "There are children in the house."

"I'll take my winnings on account. Time and place for collection to be detailed later."

"What makes you so sure you'll win?"

He waited until she was looking at him before answering. "I always win."

"So do I."

"Then that will make the game more challenging for both of us."

He thought she might protest or call him names. Instead she shrugged. He wondered if that was because she was so confident of her abilities or because she didn't mind losing.

He wanted it to be the latter. He wanted to know that she felt the tension between them as much as he did. He wanted her to want him. Something— some secret from her past—made her wary. He could accept that. He was willing to wait until she trusted him, and he would do what was necessary to earn that trust.

He took a few practice shots. His work might be intense, but there were also long hours of waiting. He'd spent a large percentage of them playing pool with his men. The rhythm of the game came back to him, and when they tossed for the break, he was confident he was going to kick butt.

D.J. won the toss and went first. As she bent over the table, he admired the lines of her strong, lean body. Just looking at her legs, at the curve of her hips and rear made him ache. He wanted to go up behind her and press himself into her. He wanted to run his hands down her back to her waist, then circle around front until he cupped her breasts. He wanted to turn her, kiss her, touch her, taste her. Take her.

He wanted her wet, willing and screaming his name. And if he acted on any of his fantasies, he was likely to get a black eye.

She called the ball and pocket, then took her shot. The ball dropped neatly into place. She lined up her second shot. With her head down, her long hair flowed over her arm. He watched the play of light on the wavy strands.

"Why do you wear it long?" he asked when she'd sunk the second ball and straightened.

"What?"

He moved close and touched her hair. "It's beautiful, but why haven't you cut it?"

D.J. told herself to move out of reach. She hated people pawing her. The thing was, having Quinn twist a strand of her hair around his finger didn't really feel all that bad. Sure he was close, but not in an aggressive, macho way.

"My mother had long hair," she said before she realized she actually intended to tell him the truth. Or at least a part of it. "When I was little, she used to brush my hair for hours, and then I would brush hers. We used to try different kinds of braids and ribbons and promise each other we'd never cut our hair short."

Quinn listened intently. His dark gaze never left her face.

"So it's worth the risk?" he asked quietly.

She nodded, knowing exactly what he meant. Long hair *was* a risk. It could be grabbed, pulled, used against her.

"I wear it braided and pinned up to my head on

assignments," she told him. It wasn't enough, but it was as much as she could do.

"Did you ever cut it?"

She nodded. "Once. I felt like I'd lost her."

The confession surprised her. She'd never told anyone that before. The realization made her nervous, but not nearly as much as the low-grade wanting she felt deep inside. She'd been waiting to see Quinn from the second she'd awakened that morning. Anticipation had slowed time to a crawl and when she'd tried to distract herself, nothing had worked.

She'd imagined what he would look like and how he would smile at her. She'd changed her clothes three times before heading over to Rebecca's. She felt giddy and foolish and tingly. Things she never allowed herself to feel.

He laced his fingers through her hair, then twisted the long strands around his hand. The action pulled slightly. Not enough to cause her pain. Another woman might not have even noticed, but D.J. did. Her senses went on alert, even as her muscles tensed.

The world blurred slightly in warning, then she was no longer in the spacious, well-lit, rec room. Instead she was a child of nine or ten. She could feel the close confines of the small space she'd squeezed into in an effort to escape. But her mother wasn't so lucky. Even as D.J. closed her eyes she could hear the screams, the pleading.

Her father had grabbed her mother by the hair. D.J. didn't remember what her mother had done that was so wrong. She could only feel her father's drunken rage. The sounds were so sharp. Her mother's voice, her father's breathing. The slick slide of the metal knife against the edge of the counter.

They'd been out of sight then, and D.J. had only been able to listen to the thunks of the blade against the cutting board. She'd heard her mother's gasps, her father's admonition to stop misbehaving. His claims that this was all *her* fault.

He'd gone back to drinking then, and had eventually passed out. D.J. remembered crawling out of her hiding space and finding her mother sitting at the kitchen table. Long, dark hair covered the cheap flooring. Her mother's hair had been hacked off unevenly. There were a few streaks of blood on her neck where the knife had cut through skin.

Her mother had never said anything about that night, nor had she tried to grow her hair back. But she'd continued to brush her daughter's hair, to braid it and tie it up in ribbons.

"D.J.?"

The light touch on her arm brought her back to the present with a stomach-clenching jolt of fear. She swung, prepared to take on her attacker, only to find herself staring at Quinn.

"Want to talk about it?" he asked quietly.

Talk about it? No. Not even a little.

"I'm fine," she told him. "Just lost in thought."

She thought he might call her on the lie, but he didn't. Still shaking a little from the flashback, she lined up her next shot and missed.

Quinn took over the table. She stayed back, watching his smooth, easy movements. When he sent the third straight ball tumbling neatly into the pocket, she got the feeling she'd been had.

"Let me guess," she said. "You've been hustling since you were a kid?"

"No. I learned in the military."

"You're good."

"Thanks."

He flashed her a grin that made her toes curl. The reaction was so unexpected, she nearly tumbled over in surprise. More to distract herself than because she wanted information, she started asking questions.

"So what was life like back in those football-star days?"

"Pretty typical small-town stuff. In Texas, high school football is practically a religion. I couldn't wait to be old enough to play. I did okay in school, drove too fast, chased girls. The usual."

His growing up hadn't been anything like her world. "You close to your folks?"

"To my mom. I never got along with the old man." He straightened. "Whatever I did wasn't good enough. I spent the first fourteen years of my life trying to figure out why he didn't love me and the next fourteen trying not to care."

"I don't understand."

Quinn shook his head. "Neither did I, until a couple of weeks ago. Apparently he and my mom couldn't have kids and he was the problem. There weren't much in the way of infertility treatments thirty-plus years ago. So he convinced her to find a guy who looked like him and get pregnant. She did and he accepted Gage as the son he never had."

D.J. hadn't thought much about how the Reynolds brothers had come to be related to the Haynes brothers. "Earl Haynes just happened to be in town?"

"Up in Dallas at a convention. My mom went

back the following year to see him. She not only found out Earl wasn't the man she thought, she ended up pregnant a second time. Her husband wasn't willing to overlook the infidelity. Eventually he forgave her, but he never forgave me.''

"Because you were a constant reminder."

"Something like that." He shrugged. "We never talked about it. He just made my life hell."

"Does knowing the reason make a difference?"

"I thought it would, but no."

D.J. could understand that. Knowing why something happened didn't always make the situation any easier to deal with. She understood everything about her past, and the knowledge was less than useless.

She couldn't see Quinn's pain, but she felt it. Oddly enough, it was something they had in common.

"My dad was a bastard, too," she told him. "Big, mean. Scary. He's the main reason I like to be in control all the time."

Confessions weren't her style and this one made her more uneasy than most. She braced herself for questions, or for him to tell her that she wasn't in control. Instead, he nodded.

"Makes sense."

He turned back to the game and continued to play perfectly. When he dropped the eight ball in the center pocket, he winked at her.

"That's gonna cost you a shirt, Daisy Jane."

"I was thinking of something more like a sock."

"It's my victory. I get to pick the item. Quit arguing or I'll make it your panties."

She reached for the rack, determined to win the second game. He broke, then promptly missed the first shot. She had a feeling he was giving her a break, but she wasn't about to complain. Not when she wanted to kick his butt and make claims on his underwear.

"When did you start learning martial arts?" he asked as she nailed her first shot.

"In high school. I worked all summer to pay for the lessons."

"I still say you would have been a terrific cheerleader."

"Oh, please. I wasn't interested in prancing around and showing off for boys."

"Some of the squads are very athletic."

She lined up the next shot. "That's true. If it had been something like that, I would have. But at my high school the girls were into looking good, not competing. I ran track."

"No archery or fencing?"

She glanced at him, but his expression was innocent enough. "It wasn't offered."

"How old were you when you earned your first black belt?"

"Seventeen."

She still remembered her pride. How she'd felt strong and safe for the first time in years.

"Did you have a boyfriend?"

She straightened. "Think about it, Quinn," she said. "I ran track, I had a black belt. What do you think?"

He walked toward her. "That you scared the boys away."

"Most of them."

He stopped next to her. "When they got too close, did you beat them up?"

She knew he was teasing and wanted to smile, but the memory of those days only made her sad. She'd never fit in. No one could understand what drove her to always want to be stronger, faster, better. She'd started to learn how to protect herself, but she'd never been able to escape being lonely.

"I didn't have to," she told him. "They never got that close."

He set his cue on the table and rested his hands on her waist. "Too bad. They should have called your bluff. Look at all they missed out on."

She didn't know what to respond to first. His closeness? She told herself to step away, but she couldn't seem to move. His comments about the past? She *hadn't* been bluffing. Her toughness had been as real as she could make it. As for missing out…did Quinn really think that? Somehow she'd always assumed the boys were never all that interested. If she wasn't girly and instantly willing, she wasn't worth the trouble.

"Quinn, I don't think this is a good idea," she told him.

"Daisy Jane, if we waited until you figured it was time, we'd both be long dead and mummified. It's up to me to move things on."

He lowered his head slightly. She could feel his breath on her cheek. "Stop calling me that."

"Sure thing, Daisy Jane."

Before she could protest or attack, he kissed her.

She'd known he was going to. How could she not? So why hadn't she bolted?

The answer became clear the second his mouth brushed against hers, sending heat flaring through her entire body.

She wanted this. She who had always prided herself on never trusting a man enough to let him get close wanted to give in. Not to any man. Just to Quinn. Just this once.

She must have dropped her cue because her hands were suddenly empty when she raised her arms and locked them around his neck. His lips were warm, firm and searching. She liked how he moved back and forth, teasing her, arousing her. Impatient for more, she parted her mouth, inviting him inside.

He responded with an eagerness that made her press against him. They touched from shoulders to knees, with her breasts flattening against his chest and her stomach nestling his rapidly growing arousal.

His tongue slipped into her mouth. She greeted him with a soft caress, then circled him. He responded in kind. The sensual contact made her breasts ache. When his hands slipped from her hips to her rear, she arched harder against him. He dug into her curves, squeezing.

His long fingers brushed against the backs of her thighs. Liquid need melted her from the inside out. He was hard to her soft—so male and powerful. The length and breadth of his erection made her wonder what he would look like naked. Every part of his body would be strong and unyielding. From there it was a short, erotic step to imagining herself on the pool table, legs spread, him filling her as they—

The image was so real, she felt a jolt deep inside. As if he'd really entered her. Passion grew, as did a steady, throbbing ache. She *wanted* him to be inside of her. She *wanted* him to touch her. If he put his fingers between her legs and rubbed against her slick, wet flesh she could…

Terror swept through her as she completed the thought. If he touched her, she would give in. She would surrender control.

"No!" she gasped as she pulled free. "Stop."

Prepared to push him away, she was surprised when he instantly stepped back.

"D.J.? What's wrong?"

"I—" She was shaking. Her chest hurt and she couldn't breathe. "I can't," she gasped, then turned and ran.

By the time she got home, she'd managed to catch her breath, but the trembling lasted for hours. She felt both frightened and embarrassed.

So Quinn had kissed her. It didn't mean anything. People kissed all the time. She'd made a big deal out of nothing.

Only it wasn't nothing to her. Quinn had asked if she'd beaten up the guys who got too close. That had never been a problem because she managed to scare them all off. Even when she hadn't meant to.

How many times had she been left alone, lonely, wondering what she'd done wrong? How many times had she wished she could trust enough to be honest, to explain why being involved was so scary for her? But no one had ever stuck around long enough for her to gather her courage. After a time, she'd stopped missing them. She'd moved on. Just as she would do when Quinn left.

She wouldn't remember him for long. He wouldn't matter. He *didn't* matter.

D.J. sat in the dark and tried to avoid the one thing she refused to admit. That she was lying about all of it. Especially about Quinn.

Chapter Nine

Quinn's cell phone rang early the next morning. As there was only one person with the number, he knew who was on the other end.

"Reynolds," he said when he'd pushed the talk button.

"Hey, Quinn."

"Major."

"How's it going?"

Quinn wasn't sure why his commanding officer was calling. Major Ron Banner didn't do social. Either he'd received the report or he'd made a decision. Quinn wasn't sure which he wanted it to be. If his boss was looking for an answer...Quinn didn't have one yet.

"I'm doing great," Quinn told him.

"Good. You're visiting family, right?"

"Yeah. Big reunion kind of thing."

"Sounds fun."

Quinn picked up his coffee. "But it's not the reason you called."

"Fair enough. The report's back."

"And?"

"The shrinks think it's a good thing you refused to take out the target. He was your former mentor, you had an emotional connection with him, and the situation wasn't life-and-death. They feel that if circumstances had been different, had he been threatening innocents, you would have taken care of him. They called it controlled resistance. It seems you have a moral code."

"Who knew," Quinn said dryly, more than able to read between the lines. Yeah, the psychologists had given him a gold star. That didn't matter squat to his CO. "You're still pissed I didn't follow orders."

"It makes my life complicated," his boss admitted. "But you know it happens."

"Because your team of assassins is a temperamental bunch?"

"Something like that. You passed on a kill. What I want to know is if it's going to happen again. The shrinks say you're ready and willing to return to the job. I'm not so sure. You still want to be a killer, Quinn?"

Those in charge, those who wrote the handbooks, passed out assignments and made sure the men were debriefed, psychoanalyzed, and kept happy used words like *targets* and *operatives*. Quinn, his boss and those on the team called it like it was.

When he wasn't busy rescuing Americans from sticky situations and honing his skills, he was moving around the world, taking out those who had been deemed undesirable. He was an assassin on the government payroll. As Ron said—a killer.

Quinn considered the question and realized he didn't have an answer. Not yet. "I don't know. I need more time."

"Take as much as you'd like. I only want you onboard if you're a hundred percent. No second-guessing, no conscience."

"Fair enough."

"You'll stay in touch?"

"Sure thing."

He heard Banner making notes in a file.

"Say another three weeks?" his boss asked.

"Fine."

Quinn disconnected the call and dropped his cell phone on the bed. In three weeks his CO would call again and ask the same question. "You still want to be a killer?" That time Quinn planned to have an answer.

Did he? Sometimes he told himself it was just a job. He was given an assignment and he carried it out. At the end of the month, he got paid. No big deal.

But lately things weren't so simple. He knew he could go back to work tomorrow and do a hell of a job. But what did that say about him? What did that make him? And did he want to be that man?

Restlessness filled him. He stood and paced the length of the room, then glanced at the clock. He was supposed to have a lesson with D.J. in an hour or so, but there was no way he could do that. Not today.

He grabbed his keys and headed out to tell her.

Fifteen minutes later he walked into her office and found her on the phone. She smiled at him, then flushed and turned away.

He remembered the pool game, the kiss and how she'd run out on him. Thinking about what went wrong had kept him up half the night. Had it just been the previous day? It felt like a lifetime ago.

He dropped his keys onto her desk and headed back to the workout room. There was a punching bag in the corner. He walked toward it, grabbing tape as he went.

After he'd shrugged out of his shirt, taped his hands and pulled on gloves, he faced the bag. He warmed up with a few easy swings. He jogged in place and stretched out muscles. As heat loosened him up, he focused on the bag and went to work.

He punched methodically, treating the bag like a person, breaking down the midsection, then going for the head. When his mind's eye told him that enemy was bloodied and broken, he mentally replaced him with someone new and fresh, then started in on him.

Energy filled him. His ability to focus allowed him to laser in on the bag. Blow after blow sent it spinning, wobbling. Sweat dripped down his face and chest. He cleared his mind of everything but the way his body moved, the power of his hits and the rhythm of his feet.

Sometime later he sensed D.J.'s presence. She hovered just at the edge of his peripheral vision. He finished the sequence, then stopped and faced her.

"I had some things to work out," he said.

She nodded.

"There won't be a lesson today."

"I understand," she said.

He wondered if she did. He wondered what she saw when she looked at him. He was normally so controlled. So careful. "Are you afraid?" he asked.

She raised her chin slightly. "Of course not."

He had the feeling that she was almost telling the truth.

He knew if he moved toward her now, while the pain and confusion was still with him, that she would back away. He would see more than fear in her eyes—he would see terror.

Who had done that to her? A parent? A boyfriend? Had she been attacked? Raped? What? There was something in her past. Something dark and ugly. It had left her scarred and broken. It had shaped who and what she was.

He supposed there were those who would be put off by the imperfection. Disgusted maybe. Not him. He wanted to know what had happened so he wouldn't make any wrong moves. He didn't want her to be afraid of him. He wanted her to feel safe.

Dumb-ass, he told himself. Like that was ever going to happen. As if he could ever be good enough for her. As if they could have something together.

He turned back to the bag and pounded it until it swung like a flag in a gale-force wind. He hit the bag over and over, until his muscles ached and he couldn't see with all the sweat burning his eyes. Until he was too tired to ask questions or care about answers.

When he stopped, she was still there. Still watching. He pulled off the gloves, then worked the tape from his hands. He sensed that she wanted to speak, and prayed she would stay silent. What was there to say?

He'd been wrong to want her, to kiss her. To like her. He'd allowed himself to forget who and what he was. A killer. A man without a soul.

His CO wanted answers, and Quinn didn't want to deal with the questions. How did he know what he wanted from life? How was he to find the best way to go? If he walked away from his job, from all of it, then what? Could he find his way back to normal? Did he even remember what that was?

All those people last night at Rebecca's house. They'd been family, yet they were strangers. Even Gage. None of them knew what he did, who he was. If he walked away, could he be a part of them? Did he want to be?

He grabbed his shirt and brushed his damp hair off his forehead.

"I'll see you around," he told her.

D.J. nodded without speaking.

He wanted to explain, but what was there to say? He was going to find high ground, hole up and lick his wounds. He was a solitary creature and no matter what else he wanted, that wasn't going to change.

That afternoon D.J. tried to focus on paperwork, but she was having trouble concentrating. She kept thinking about Quinn, about what had happened that morning.

She'd dreaded their session together because of the kiss at Rebecca's and her reaction to it. She'd wanted to be cool and sophisticated. She'd wanted to impress him. Passion had threatened to overwhelm her and she'd bolted like a scared schoolgirl.

She'd tried to think of a reason to cancel their session. Before she could come up with one, he'd stalked into the office, looking exactly like what he was—a dangerous man. Something in his eyes had made her want to get out of his way. Suddenly the kiss didn't matter. Not when she had to face down a warrior.

He hadn't worked out on her punching bag, he'd attacked it, as if it possessed demons. She could still hear the sound of his gloves hitting the bag. The steady thumps, the low grunts of effort, the shuffle of his feet on the floor.

Something had happened, but she didn't know what. Something had set him off. At first she'd thought they could spar together and he would deal with whatever was bothering him. But after she'd seen him at the punching bag, she'd known that wasn't possible. He'd become too deadly.

D.J. stood and walked out of the office. After locking the front door, she crossed the small parking lot to her SUV and climbed inside. When Quinn had walked out that morning, she'd thought he looked…alone. Crazy, she told herself. If Quinn was a solitary person, it was by choice. But she couldn't shake the notion that he'd been feeling isolated and separate—sensations she was intimately familiar with.

She drove through town but not toward her place. She wasn't ready to go home—not yet. She cruised past the shopping mall, a park, several restaurants before finding herself in front of Quinn's hotel.

Without knowing if it was smart or right or even safe, she pulled in and parked. Ten minutes of considering options didn't clear her mind or give her any ideas.

Cursing both him and herself, she climbed out and headed for the three-story building. Minutes later she knocked on his hotel room.

The door opened. He'd showered since she'd last seen him, and had changed his clothes. But he hadn't recovered. There was still something dark and bruised lurking in his eyes.

He didn't speak. Nor did he shut the door in her face. Instead he stepped back to let her enter.

She did. When he closed the door behind her, she decided to be completely honest.

"I don't know why I'm here," she said.

He wore a T-shirt tucked into jeans. He was lean, muscled and broken. She couldn't explain the latter, but she felt it down to her toes. Something inside of him had shattered.

The thought of his pain propelled her across the carpeting. She walked up to him, put her hands on his shoulders, raised herself on tiptoe and kissed him.

She couldn't explain her actions or predict his response. Before she could pull back or even call herself a name for being so stupid, his arms came around her and hauled her against him.

One second she was standing, the next she was pressed against him, her breasts flat against his chest, her fingers tunneling through his hair.

His hands were everywhere. Her back, her hips, her rear. Even as he tilted his head and swept his tongue across her bottom lip, his fingers brushed against her stomach before reaching higher.

She parted and he plunged inside. He circled her

tongue, claimed it, then retreated and bit her lower lip. As she gasped with surprise and a jolt of passion, she felt his hands cup her breasts. He explored the full curves. Fingertips danced across her tight nipples. He flicked the tips with his thumb. At the same time he drew her lower lip into his mouth and sucked where he'd bitten her.

Wanting overwhelmed her. Her heart rate increased, as did the sound of the blood rushing through her body. Between her legs moist warmth invaded, making her slick, swollen and ready. She wanted to rub against him like a cat. She wanted to purr. Instead she ran her hands up and down his back, reveling in his strength, his maleness.

He tugged at the front of her shirt, pulling the fabric from her jeans. Even as he kissed her jaw, her neck, then licked and bit her earlobe, he worked the buttons free. When he shoved it down her arms and tossed it on the floor, he dropped his hands to her hips and drew her pelvis against him. He was aroused and he ground himself against her.

She caught her breath and found herself lost in his dark gaze. Passion tightened the lines of his face. He wanted her and his need increased her own.

Still staring at her face, he slipped his hands up her back to her bra. With nimble fingers he unfastened the clasp. The plain cotton bra fell down her arms, and she let it fall to the floor.

He dropped his gaze to her chest. She watched him watch her as he cupped her bare breasts in his hands. When he bent low, she braced herself for the sensual assault of his kiss. Seconds later firm lips claimed her right nipple. Liquid fire roared through

her. Her head fell back as he licked and sucked her
sensitive skin.

Her thighs trembled. She had to hold on to him
to stay standing. Every cell in her body delighted in
his touch and the promise of what was to come.

Without warning, he bent low and wrapped his
arms around her legs. He picked her up and carried
her the few feet to the bed. But instead of straight-
ening after he set her down, he dropped to his knees
and went to work on her jeans.

He quickly unfastened the belt, then undid the
single button and the zipper. When he'd pulled the
fabric down to her knees, he leaned in and kissed
her flat belly.

D.J.'s entire body clenched. She couldn't part her
legs, nor could she run. When he pulled down her
panties, she stopped breathing. When he used his
fingers to delicately open her, then touched her most
sensitive place with his tongue, she had to grit her
teeth to keep from screaming.

One stroke, then two. Muscles rippled. Heat grew.
The need, oh, how the need filled her until it was
impossible to think of anything else.

"Wait," she breathed, and sank back on the bed.
"One of us is too formally dressed."

Quinn looked at her. Some of the darkness had
faded from his eyes and he smiled. "Fair enough."

He stood and tugged off his T-shirt. While he
worked on the rest of his clothing, she took off her
shoes, socks, jeans and briefs. Kneeling on the bed,
she reached for her braid and began to unfasten the
thick plait.

Quinn swore.

She looked up and saw him standing, jeans open,

feet and chest bare. His gaze roamed her body. He swore again.

She realized she was kneeling naked on his bed, her legs spread, her arms up. Aware of her vulnerability, she waited for apprehension to chill her enthusiasm, but it never came. Instead she felt proud that he found her attractive.

He shook his head. "You're a hell of a fantasy, D.J."

He shoved down his jeans and briefs as he spoke. His arousal sprang free.

He was large, thick and more than ready. She did her best not to think about what it would feel like when he was inside. Instead she finished loosening her braid, then tossed her head. He made a noise low in his throat and dove onto the bed.

He crashed next to her, brought his arms around her and pulled her down. Their mouths met in a hot, frenzied kiss that made her strain against him. He caressed her breasts, then slipped lower to the swollen wetness between her thighs.

The second he touched her there, she knew she was in trouble. The wanting was too great. Need made her whimper and squirm and surge toward him.

Just for a second, she told herself, trying to stay in control. She would let him do this just for a second. It felt so good. Too good to make him stop.

He moved slowly, as if discovering. When he brushed across her most sensitive spot, she caught her breath. He did it again and again. She could feel herself tensing, readying. So close. If he didn't stop, she wouldn't have a choice.

Deliberately she put her hand on his wrist and

pushed him away. At the same time, she clamped her lips over his tongue and sucked until he shuddered.

Pulling back slightly she said, ''Tell me you have protection with you because I don't.''

''What?'' His dark eyes were unfocused. He blinked, then grinned. ''Sure thing, Daisy Jane.''

She swatted his arm. ''Stop calling me that.''

''Why? It's your name.''

He rose and walked into the bathroom. Seconds later he appeared with a box of condoms. He tossed them onto the nightstand, then returned to the bed. She knew what he planned even before he slipped his hand between her legs.

''Wait,'' she told him. ''I want you ready.''

Quinn started to protest, but before he could get up a head of steam, she bent down and took him in her mouth. He groaned low in his throat. As she teased him with her tongue, she reached for the box of condoms.

When he was breathing heavily and sagging against the bed, she raised her head and opened the box. He watched her slip on the protection.

Before he could shift toward her, she knelt over him and slowly settled on his arousal. He grabbed her hips.

''D.J., wait,'' he gasped. ''I want you to—''

She sank lower. ''I will,'' she told him. ''Just let's get you going.''

''I'm already there.''

She smiled and slowly raised and lowered herself over his arousal.

He felt good, she thought, holding on to her control. Too good. It would be easy to give in to the feelings surging through her. But she couldn't. So she concentrated on letting him slip in and out of her, squeezing him with each stroke. The fingers on her hips tightened as he began to set the pace.

He moved one hand across her leg so he could reach her wetness. Even as she rode him, he rubbed his thumb against her swollen center.

Exquisite pleasure shot through her. She wanted to collapse against him, surrendering to the release. She was so close. Just a few more strokes. Just a few more...

No! She forced her mind away from what he was doing between her legs. Instead of letting go, she breathed his name. He opened his eyes and looked at her. While he watched, she gathered her hair and piled it on top of her head. The movement of her arms raised her breasts. She began to move faster and faster, pulling him inside of her. Her breasts bounced, her body rode him, she tightened her muscles, milking him until she felt him stiffen.

He swore again and replaced his thumb with two fingers. His pace matched hers. She was sliding over the edge. Control, she thought frantically. Control.

She dropped her hands to the mattress and pulsed her hips. The shift in her position forced his hand away and pulled him in deeper. At the apex of the thrust, she clamped around him and rocked.

He lost it.

Contentment filled her as she felt him shudder in release. His eyes sank closed, his body stiffened, then stilled. Between her thighs she felt the contractions slow, slow and finally stop.

She sighed and smiled. "Impressive," she breathed.

Quinn opened his eyes. For a man who'd just had what felt like an amazing climax, he didn't look happy. Instead of smiling back, he grabbed her and shifted so she tumbled onto her back. Then he loomed over her.

''What the hell just happened?'' he growled.

Chapter Ten

Quinn stared into D.J.'s face, but couldn't figure out what she was thinking. Her smile faded.

"What's wrong?" she asked.

She seemed genuinely confused.

He mentally grabbed hold of his temper. Okay, maybe he'd misread the situation. Maybe she hadn't done it on purpose.

"You had your way with me," he said, deliberately lightening his tone. "What's up with that?"

Her smile returned. "I wanted it to be good for you."

"What about you?"

"It was fine."

"Uh-huh."

He didn't believe her for a second. She'd held back. If he didn't know better, he would say she'd been damn close but had tried to distract him. Tried? She'd succeeded. But why?

To test his theory, he slipped a hand between her legs. She was wet, hot and more than swollen. He found the tight knot of nerves and rubbed it with his finger. Instantly her breath quickened and her pupils dilated.

But instead of letting him continue, she pushed his hand away and sat up. "Like I said—impressive."

She started to slide off the bed, but he grabbed her arm and held her in place. "What's going on?" he demanded a second time.

"Nothing." She narrowed her gaze. "Would you please let go of me?"

"When you tell me why this whole exercise was about me."

"Isn't that what you want?"

"No. I want it to be about both of us."

"It's sex, Quinn. Nothing more."

"I would have enjoyed sex. This was getting off."

She flushed and turned away. He released her arm and watched her stand up. She was more beautiful than he could have imagined. Strong, curved, completely feminine. From her high breasts to the triangle of dark curls protecting her femininity, she was erotic, sensual and pure fantasy.

She'd shocked him when she'd shown up at his door. He'd almost told her to leave, but he'd been tired of being alone. Then she'd kissed him and he'd realized why she'd come to see him. What she was offering. Somehow he'd assumed it would be for both of them.

He pulled off the condom and tossed it in the trash, then watched her gather her clothes. She pulled on briefs and her bra. As she stepped into her jeans, he tried to figure out what had gone wrong.

Her lack of reaction hadn't been about his technique. He might not be God's gift to women, but he understood basic anatomy. He knew what went where and did his best to always make his partner see stars. But D.J. hadn't let him. Every time he'd been close, she'd pulled back.

"You're not leaving until this is settled," he told her.

She eyed him coolly. "You're going to keep me prisoner?"

"If necessary."

"Big talk from a naked guy." She shrugged into her shirt and fastened the buttons.

"Is it a control thing?" he asked.

She tucked her shirt into her jeans. "I have no idea what you're talking about."

"You could have climaxed. You were close. I could feel it. So what's the deal?"

She walked to the mirror over the dresser and finger combed her hair. "There's no deal."

Like he bought that. "Control?" he asked, speaking more to himself than her. "But what's the point? So you don't enjoy sex. How is that a win?"

She spun to face him. "You got yours, Quinn. Isn't that enough?"

"No." He stood and put his hands on his hips. "It's not how I do things."

"So if she's not screaming your name, you're not a man?"

"Something like that."

"Well, get over it. What happened today, or didn't happen, wasn't about you. It was about me. I don't—" she turned back to the mirror "—I'm not built that way. My body doesn't react."

He grabbed his jeans and pulled them on. "Are you telling me you've never had a climax? That you're incapable?"

"Yes." She turned back to him. "It happens."

"Bull. You're more in tune with your body than anyone I've ever met. I felt you reacting, D.J. You were close. You deliberately pulled back."

Her dark eyes flashed with temper. "Maybe you're overestimating your skill in bed."

"I don't claim to be the world's greatest lover. I'm just a guy who wants to please the one he's with. What's so wrong with that."

She sighed. "Nothing. I appreciate the thought, but it's not necessary."

"It is to me."

"This isn't about you."

He crossed to her and touched her chin. When she looked at him, he smiled. "I've got all night. Let's get naked again and we'll see if I can prove you wrong."

She twisted away from him. "Thanks, but I'm not interested."

"Then why did you show up in the first place?"

"Good question. I'm having some second thoughts."

He frowned. None of this made sense. She'd arrived uninvited and had taken the first step. *She'd* kissed *him.* When he'd responded, she'd been more than willing. She'd wanted to have sex, but only if it was about him.

What was that?

She headed for the door. He got there first. "Answer the question," he said quietly. "Tell me why you won't let me make you climax and I'll let it go."

She sucked in a breath, then released it slowly. "I'm not interested in—" She shook her head. "You're so annoying."

"I know. Answer the question."

She looked at him. "I just don't. Okay? It's not that I can't, it's that I won't. Doing that..." She shrugged. "I won't ever let myself be that vulnerable."

If she'd screamed he wouldn't have believed her. But it was her soft words, the defensive set of her shoulders and the painful twist of her mouth that convinced him.

He stared at her. "Why do you hate men so much?"

"I don't. It's not about hating anyone. That implies way more energy than I'm putting into this."

She turned away and crossed to the bed. Once there, she sank onto the mattress.

"It's about not trusting them," she told him. "Sex does something to women. It makes them weak. They bond. And it doesn't seem to matter if the guy's a jerk or not. Or if he beats her. They connect. I don't want to be that weak, so I don't risk it."

Her words stunned him. "Not ever?"

"What's the point? You get weak, you get dead."

"That's ridiculous. You're extrapolating from an inconsequential statistical base. How many women get dead because they have sex?"

She sprang to her feet. "One woman is too many. You're a guy. You don't know what you're talking about."

"Then tell me. Help me understand."

She shook her head and crossed to the door. This time he knew he had to let her go. But she surprised him by laying her hand against the wood frame rather than the handle.

"My father beat my mother," she said, her back to him. "He was a mean drunk and even worse when he was sober. My earliest memory is of her screaming for mercy."

Quinn's stomach clenched. He'd wanted to know what had so terrified D.J. Now that he did, he wanted to rescind the request. Knowing didn't make it better.

"Sometimes he would go days, even a couple of weeks between attacks. I'd lie awake every night, wondering if it would start. When it would start. I was always afraid. What if he killed her? What if he turned on me, too."

She dropped her hand to her side, then shifted so she was facing him. "He waited until my seventh birthday. He got drunk, I spilled cake on the floor and he came after me. Sometimes he used a belt or his hand. He'd throw beer bottles at me. Then he'd pass out. When it was finally safe, my mother and I would huddle together on the sofa and make plans to escape. For a long time I believed that it was really going to happen."

Her dark eyes stared past him. Was she getting lost in the memories? Would she let him help her?

"She changed her mind," D.J. told him. "Every time. The next morning there were a thousand reasons why we couldn't go. The truth was, she loved him. Even when he broke her jaw, cut off her hair and called her a whore.''

He wanted to go to her and hold her but knew she wouldn't want to be touched. Not now. Not when it wasn't safe.

She closed her eyes. ''When I was eleven he came after me with a baseball bat. I can't even remember why. Just how bad it hurt. My mother took me to the emergency room. My arm was broken. The nurse there threatened to call the police and have me taken away. My mother begged her not to. She said my father would kill me if the police got involved. The nurse said he was going to kill me anyway.''

She opened her eyes and stared at him. ''My mother took me home and told me it would be all right. The next day she made me go to school. I didn't want to. I was ashamed and in a lot of pain. But she insisted. The school nurse came and got me later that morning. After I'd left home that morning, my mother shot my father, then turned the gun on herself. She left a note. In it she said she couldn't let him continue to hurt me, but she couldn't live knowing she'd killed the only man she ever loved.''

He swallowed hard. D.J. stood by the door, rubbing her left arm. He didn't doubt those bones had been the ones shattered.

He'd already guessed she'd been abused in some way, but he'd never thought it was that bad. No wonder she didn't trust men or love or sex. No wonder she held back.

''I'm sorry,'' he said. ''I shouldn't have asked.''

Her mouth twisted. ''More than you wanted to know, huh?''

He stood. "There's nothing you can say that will shock me. I'm sorry for making you relive it."

She shrugged. "Old news. It doesn't matter anymore."

Of course it mattered. Her past dictated every aspect of her life. It was the reason she had to always be the best. He ached for her.

"D.J."

She held up a hand. "If you get all sloppy on me, I'm going to beat the crap out of you."

"Not a chance of that."

He crossed the room and reached for her. She shrank back, then stiffened and stood her ground. He'd seen men in battle, facing down their fear, but not one of them had shown the same courage as this woman. Every time he moved, she knew he could snap her in two. Yet instead of running for cover, she wanted him to teach her. When she could have walked away, she'd come over to help him heal. She had seen the nature of the darkness inside of him that morning. She'd watched him pulverize the punching bag, and she'd still shown up and offered herself.

"You're a hell of a woman," he said as he put his arms around her and pulled her close.

She was stiff as plywood. "I don't need a hug."

"Maybe I do."

She sighed heavily, as if this was *such* an imposition, then stood there while he ran his hands up and down her back. Gradually she began to relax. Her arms moved from her sides to his waist. Her fingers lightly rested against his back.

He breathed in the scent of her body, of her hair. She was tough, but still soft. He understood why she hadn't given in. He also finally knew why offering him sex in exchange for lessons had been so much easier than accepting a dinner invitation. Sex was just about the body. She could stay in control—although she'd come close to losing it with him. Dinner was more personal.

He also knew what had gone wrong between them today. She'd offered sex, and he'd accepted. Neither of them had been making love.

Quinn's chest tightened. Was that what he wanted? To make love with D.J.? Did he dare?

She pulled away and this time he let her go. She crossed to the door and let herself out without saying anything.

When her footsteps had faded, he moved to the window and stared out. He saw her walk across the parking lot and slide into her car. She moved with a grace that left him breathless.

He still wanted her, and he knew what it would take to get her. But could he risk it? He was the wrong man to try to save her. She might be on the edge, but he was already in the water and drowning.

She started her engine and drove away. Even after she was gone, he stayed at the window. Was it wishful thinking on his part to hope they could save each other? Were they both too far gone or did they have a prayer of finding their way back?

The next morning D.J. waited nervously for Quinn to arrive. Part of her hoped he wouldn't bother. That between what had happened—or not happened—in bed and their fight, he'd decided to forget it. His not showing up would make things easy for her. No more worries, no more questions, no more second-guessing herself.

She hadn't slept at all the previous night. Her feelings had fluctuated between anger, humiliation and frustration. She couldn't believe she'd simply blurted out the truth about her past. She never told anyone. Rebecca didn't even know. Oh, there had been hints, but she'd never actually sat down and spilled the whole sorry tale.

D.J. paced the length of her office, then returned to her desk and flopped down on the chair. Why had she told him? She wanted to say it was because he kept pushing and pushing, but she wasn't sure. Part of her wondered if she'd *wanted* him to know.

"Not possible," she said aloud. Him knowing only complicated an already difficult situation. Unless she'd been trying to scare him off.

She rose again and nodded. That was it. She'd wanted to send Quinn away.

Or had she wanted him to understand?

The question terrified her and she refused to consider it. No way. Not possible. Uh-uh. Him understanding would imply that he mattered, and he didn't. She'd proved that yesterday when they'd had sex. She'd held back the way she always did. The only difference was he'd noticed.

She crossed to the window and stared out at the street. Half the men she'd been with hadn't even wondered about her enjoying the process or not. A few had been worried, but she'd brushed them off. The rest she'd convinced that they'd simply missed her "event." Quinn had been the only one to push back.

She closed her eyes as she remembered his anger

and his persistence. What he didn't know—what she would never tell him—was how close she'd come to giving in. She'd wanted to, and that realization scared her to death.

Her eyes snapped open. "What's up with all this Quinn crap?" she demanded of herself. "Stop thinking about him."

Good advice she couldn't seem to take. While his badgering had been annoying, she had to admit that it had been sweet of him to care so much. He'd—

She turned and glanced at the clock. It was nine. Maybe he wasn't coming.

She told herself she would be relieved if he didn't show up. Better for both of them to end things now. Not that there was anything to end. But if there was, it should stop immediately. Yes, the lessons had been great but—

The front door opened. D.J. turned and ignored the sense of relief that swept through her when Quinn entered the room. Her gaze swept over him, taking in his easy smile, the athletic shorts and T-shirt, the flowers in his hand, the way he—

Her gaze snapped back to the flowers. Outrage filled her. "What the hell are those?" she demanded.

"Good morning to you, too," he said and put the dozen or so red roses on her desk.

She couldn't believe it. He'd brought her flowers?

"Of all the insensitive, stupid things you could have done," she told him, her temper growing by the second. "Flowers? You brought me flowers? Oh, right. Because they're going to make up for everything that's happened. Gee, I should have thought of that kind of therapy before. A few flowers will really heal my past.''

She walked around the desk and glared at him. ''Were you even listening to what I said yesterday? Don't you think this ridiculous gesture trivializes the story just a little bit? Or should I be grateful you thought about it at all? How like a man.''

She wanted to squash him like a bug. She wanted to shove the roses in his face until he choked on them.

''You have no idea what I went through,'' she continued angrily. ''You grew up in some perfect hometown where everyone knew your name. I was stuck in foster care because my mother killed my father and then herself. Imagine what the kids at school talked about when I walked into a room. The teachers kept waiting for me to explode or something, and there was an entire team of psychologists trying to make sure I was healed. Well here's a news flash. You don't heal from something like that. You learn to live with it and then you move on.''

Quinn didn't move, didn't stop smiling at her, didn't say a word until she'd wound down enough to demand, ''What?''

He nodded at the flowers. ''They have nothing to do with your past. I always bring flowers after I see a woman naked. It seems like the polite thing to do. I ordered them just for you. They still have their thorns. I thought you'd like that.''

D.J.'s mouth dropped open. She closed it, then felt herself flush.

She was an idiot. ''Oh.''

''Is that it?''

She shrugged.

"How about thanking me?" he asked. "The thorns are a pretty cool touch."

She smiled. "They are. Thank you."

Quinn shook his head. "Okay, I say we start the workout with you spending about twenty minutes jumping rope. You have way too much energy you need to burn off."

D.J. nodded and led the way toward the back. He followed. When they stepped into the workout room, he grabbed her hand and pulled her around so she faced him.

"Are we okay?" he asked.

He'd brought her flowers. No guy had ever done that before. Not that she *needed* flowers, but it had been sweet of him to go to all that trouble.

"I'm sorry I overreacted," she said.

"Is that a yes?"

"Yes."

"Good. But don't think apologizing gets you out of jumping rope." He released her hand. "Get going."

She grinned and headed for the equipment locker. Maybe telling him about her past hadn't been such a big mistake. Maybe everything was going to work out just fine.

A week later D.J. couldn't figure out if things were better or worse between herself and Quinn. While he'd never mentioned that night, the sex or her confession, she couldn't convince herself he'd forgotten anything that had happened or anything she'd said. Or maybe she was giving him more credit than he deserved. Maybe *she* was the problem. Because ever since they'd done the wild thing and she'd spilled her emotional guts, she'd been far too *aware* of him.

When they worked out, she noticed every brush of his hand, ever whisper of masculine scent. When they talked, she studied his conversation for nuance and hidden meaning. Yes, she was getting stronger and learning more about keeping safe than she'd hoped, but she was also being driven to distraction by his presence.

"So stop thinking about him," she told herself as she turned in front of Rebecca's house and walked to the front door.

Her friend let her in before she could knock.

"I was watching for you," Rebecca said. "I sent the kids out with Austin, so it's just us for lunch." She smiled. "I thought about having doughnuts, in honor of our temporarily halted morning tradition, but that was just too strange for an actual meal."

"I wouldn't have minded," D.J. told her as she followed her back to the kitchen. "You know, you didn't have to stop coming by and visiting me."

Rebecca crossed the kitchen, pausing by the island where she'd already put out ingredients for salad. "Of course I did. Whatever we have to say to each other can wait until we get together for lunch or talk on the phone. This is the first time I've ever seen you interested in a man. I'm not getting in the way of that. You know where everything is. Help yourself to whatever you want to drink."

"Thanks." D.J. headed for the cupboard beside the dishwasher and pulled out a glass. "Just for the record, I'm not interested in Quinn."

Rebecca grinned. "Just for the record, you're lying."

D.J. ignored her and walked to the refrigerator. After filling her glass with ice, she opened the door and pulled out a diet soda.

Interest implied that she wanted something from Quinn, and she didn't. Not really. Okay, he confused her and she couldn't stop thinking about him, but that didn't mean he was important to her in any way. He was just…confusing.

"He's not sticking around," she reminded her friend. "His stay in town is temporary."

Rebecca cut up an avocado. "What does that have to do with anything?"

"If you're pushing for us to have a relationship, I'm telling you that it would have to be temporary."

"Not necessarily. He won't be staying in the military forever."

Good point. "He's not my type."

"You don't date enough to have a type."

Another good point. "Enough about me. Let's talk about you. How are the kids?"

Rebecca grated cheese over the salad, then handed the bowl to D.J. "Please take that to the table and don't for a second think you can change the subject. The kids are fine, Austin is fine, and I'm fine. Now, back to you and Quinn."

"There is no 'me and Quinn.' There's just me."

"So the fact that I see his rental car at your office every morning is insignificant?"

"Absolutely. He's working out with me, that's all."

Rebecca uncovered a plate of sandwiches and set them next to the salad. "Half-dressed sweaty bodies rolling around together? It sounds romantic to me."

"Then you need to work on your definitions." D.J. slumped down in a chair.

Rebecca sat across from her.

They couldn't be more opposite, D.J. thought. Rebecca wore a light, summer dress, jewelry and a bow in her hair. D.J. had pulled on khaki pants, a tank top and sandals. The closest she came to jewelry was the sports watch she sometimes remembered to strap on. Her hair was pulled back because that kept it out of her way. She felt as feminine and delicate as a machine gun.

Rebecca wore makeup, painted her nails, baked, sewed her kids Halloween costumes and acted as room mother in all her children's classrooms. D.J. had three black belts, no family and not even a houseplant to act as a pet.

Sometimes, not often, but sometimes, she wanted more. She wanted to be normal—like the other women she saw. Sometimes she wondered how her life would have been different if she hadn't grown up afraid. If she'd never learned that men couldn't be trusted.

"What are you thinking?" Rebecca asked as she scooped salad onto her plate. "You're looking fierce."

"I'm wondering how you can do all this without being afraid."

Rebecca frowned. "Of what?"

"Men. What they can do to women. How much stronger they are."

"I'll admit there are criminals out there, and bad men, but they're not a part of our everyday life. We don't live in a war zone, D.J. Sometimes I think you forget that."

"Maybe."

"You see the worst side of people. In your class you help women who have been abused or battered. While I admire what you do, it doesn't give you a balanced view of humanity."

"You want balanced? How about the percentage of woman who are beaten by their husbands? Or the kids who—"

Rebecca raised her hand. "That's my point. You live in a world of statistics. Of bad things. But most of us don't. We have regular lives with great guys. Oh, sure, they can be annoying but they're still honest, caring men. They're good parents and would rather cut off their own arms than hurt their wives or kids."

D.J. wanted to believe her. She knew in her head that most men weren't the enemy. The problem was, she didn't seem to run into many of them.

She wondered what her friend would say if she knew what had happened that night in Quinn's hotel room. Rebecca would be far more shocked by D.J.'s inability to let go than by the fact that she'd had sex. No doubt Rebecca assumed D.J.'s physical prowess extended into the bedroom. Most people probably thought that.

"There's too much surrender in marriage, and it all happens on the woman's part."

Rebecca bit into her sandwich and chewed. "I disagree," she said when she'd swallowed. "Both partners surrender. And with the right man it can be a wonderful thing."

"Oh, please."

"It's true. Being vulnerable and open to a man, while he's vulnerable and open to you, is the purest form of connection. Each of you can hurt the other, and you don't. That's what love is. Sharing secrets, trusting. Trust is the proof of love. Without it love doesn't exist.''

''I'm not interested in love.''

''Of course you are,'' Rebecca said quietly. ''But the fear is greater than the wanting. I've always thought that was sad. I want you to find someone and be happy.''

D.J. bristled. ''I don't need some man to make me happy.''

''Maybe not, but you need someone to crawl inside of you and prove that you can stop running.''

D.J. poked at her salad. ''This is a stupid conversation.''

''Quinn's an interesting guy.''

''None of this is about him.''

Rebecca smiled. ''Of course it isn't. As you said—he's leaving soon. Of course he would be someone good for you to practice on. So when the right one came along, you'd know what to do.''

''There is no right one.''

Rebecca's smile broadened. ''For a woman who thinks she knows everything, you're surprisingly ignorant of matters of the heart.''

''What do you mean by that?''

''You're already falling for him, D.J. I can see it from here.''

''No way. He doesn't matter.'' He didn't. He couldn't. She didn't let anyone matter. Not ever.

''Sell it somewhere else.''

D.J. ignored her. There was nothing going on between her and Quinn. Okay—they'd had sex, but so what? It had been a week and he hadn't tried to do it again. Which was how she preferred things. The last thing she needed was some guy pawing her. It was disgusting. She much preferred being alone. At least she always had…until lately.

Chapter Eleven

"I can't believe we're doing this," D.J. told him as he held open the heavy glass door.

"I know. It's pretty special."

Quinn glanced around at the mall. He couldn't remember the last time he'd been in a suburban shopping center. Whenever he had to buy a gift— usually for his mother at Christmas or her birthday—he used the Internet.

The Glenwood Mall had been recently refurbished. Skylights flooded the two-story structure with plenty of light. While there were a few families out and about, most of the occupants seemed to be teenagers and retired couples. An interesting mix.

"You tricked me," D.J. said with a laugh.

Quinn turned his attention back to her and grinned. "I told you I was more than just a pretty face."

She rolled her eyes. "I wasn't kidding about shopping."

"That's fine."

"Won't going into a store give you hives or something? Don't all guys hate to shop?"

"I don't do it very often. I think I can survive any autoimmune-system reaction. If I don't, I'm sure you know first aid."

Her gaze narrowed. "Just don't expect mouth-to-mouth."

He snapped his fingers. "Bummer. I had this whole fantasy about keeling over in men's wear."

"I'm sure one of the burly guards would be happy to save your life."

"I'd rather you did it."

She shook her head and walked to the directory. Quinn followed. When he'd invited D.J. to dinner, he'd expected her to blow him off. But instead of refusing him outright, she'd said she had to shop for Rebecca's birthday. When he'd offered to accompany her *and* buy her dinner, she'd accepted. He'd been surprised and she'd looked a little stunned herself. Still, he considered her agreement progress. Not that D.J. made anything easy.

"You want to shop first or eat?" he asked.

"Where are we eating?"

"The food court."

She looked at him and blinked. "You're kidding?"

He put a hand on her arm. "I know it's going to be exciting for you, but try to control yourself. It gets embarrassing when you scream and jump all over me."

"The food court?"

"Sure. I'll let you have anything you want, and you can even have ice cream for dessert."

"I'm overwhelmed."

He grinned. "I thought you might be. And if any of the teenage boys try to hit on you, I'll scare them off."

She smiled. "I can't imagine anything more wonderful."

He tucked his hands into the front pockets of his jeans. "I do know how to show a lady a good time."

"Gee, with all that to look forward to, I guess we should shop first and let the anticipation build."

"That's my girl."

D.J. mumbled something under her breath. Quinn thought it best not to ask her to repeat it.

She led the way into a large department store. The main floor was a maze of cosmetics, women's shoes and jewelry. Quinn thought he caught sight of the men's department tucked into a far corner, but he wasn't sure and D.J. didn't head in that direction. Instead she circled the cosmetics, then hovered around the perfume counter.

"I never know what to get Rebecca," she admitted. "We had lunch yesterday and I kept looking at her, thinking we have absolutely nothing in common."

"So get something you'd hate, and she'll probably love it."

D.J. shook her head. "Gee, thanks for the advice."

She picked up a cut-glass bottle and sniffed, then grimaced and put it back down. Quinn understood her concern. From what he could tell the only thing similar about Rebecca and D.J. was that they were both female. But the relationship didn't surprise him. Rebecca provided D.J. with balance, although he doubted Miss Prickly would ever admit to it.

"She's so girly," D.J. muttered. "It's just…"

She didn't want to get it wrong. Quinn didn't have to hear the words to know what she was thinking. She might rag on Rebecca, but she cared about her. D.J. didn't let many people into her world, but when she did, they were in for life.

He wondered where he was on her radar. Not the inner circle. But someone she trusted—at least a little. She'd been willing to get naked with him, which meant a lot, even if she hadn't been willing to let herself enjoy the experience. Even more telling, she'd told him about her past.

Quinn still didn't know what to do with the information. Her old man was dead, so finding him and beating the crap out of him wasn't an option, although it had been his first response. He had no patience for those who preyed on the small and weak. If a man wanted to pick a fight, he should do it with someone his own size.

He knew that D.J.'s past had left her broken, and not just in her bones. He wanted to pull her close until she healed. Yeah, right. Because he was so mentally sound himself.

"Let's check out some of the boutiques," she said, leading the way out of the anchor store.

"What does Rebecca like?" he asked. "What about shoes? Aren't all women into shoes?"

D.J. raised her eyebrows. "Have you ever bought shoes for a woman."

"No."

"I suggest you never try."

"Fair enough."

He glanced down at her feet. She wore sandals. He liked looking at her bare feet. But with D.J. he pretty much liked looking at bare anything. Even in jeans and a tank top, which she had on tonight, she was sexy as hell. He wanted her naked, in his bed and screaming out her pleasure. As this was his fantasy and unlikely to happen anytime soon, he added the thrill of her grabbing him by the hips and begging him to take her.

"You're grinning," she said. "What are you thinking?"

"You really want to know?"

She sighed. "Probably not."

They passed a lingerie store. "What about something from here?" he asked. "I could get into that."

"How typical."

"Men are more visual than women. It's not our fault."

"Uh-huh." She paused outside a music box store. "They had a couple of things in here I saw last month, but I don't know."

Quinn moved behind her. The window display had been filled with music boxes. Everything from china dogs to dolls to carved wooden boxes.

"It seems like a Rebecca kind of place," he said.

D.J. shrugged. "The stuff in here is too impractical."

She started to walk away but he grabbed her arm. "Wait. Don't you want to look inside?"

"Maybe."

Her brown eyes darkened with something he didn't recognize at first. Then he recognized vulnerability.

He rubbed his thumb against her upper arm. "If it's from you, she's going to love it."

"You don't know that."

"Actually, I do. Rebecca loves you."

D.J. squirmed free. "We're friends."

"That's what I said."

She muttered something he couldn't hear and stalked into the store. Quinn wondered why the *L* word bothered her so much. As a guy he could understand not wanting to hear it in a romantic sense. There was the whole being-trapped feeling. Although he'd never minded the thought of one woman for the rest of his life. But weren't women supposed to be the warm nurturing ones? Didn't love come easy for them, especially between friends?

Then he reminded himself this was D.J., and while she might be sexy and the most challenging woman he'd ever met, she wasn't even close to easy.

He followed her into the store. She'd stopped in front of a display of tropical music boxes. One had a colorful cloisonné butterfly on top. She touched the edge of the wing.

"It's beautiful," he told her.

"It reminds me of Rebecca."

"I can see that." Oddly enough, it also reminded him of D.J., who was beautiful, but also tough. Like the butterflies who migrated thousands of miles each year.

She sighed. "I guess I'll get it. I mean, I don't see anything else I like as well."

She was acting like this was no big deal, but he'd already figured out the truth. D.J. had wanted to buy the music box for Rebecca from the moment she'd seen it. But for some reason she'd been worried it wasn't perfect. So she'd waited to get someone else's opinion. He was touched that she'd allowed him to be the one to help her decide.

"She'll love it," he said.

"I hope so."

Without thinking, he reached out and lightly stroked her cheek. She looked at him.

"What do you think you're doing?" she asked.

"Touching you."

"Why?"

"Because I want to."

Her eyes widened slightly. Tension crackled between them. Sure there was sexual awareness, but there was also something more. A connection. A possibility.

He waited for her to pull back, to protest, to slap his hand away. Instead she smiled.

"Okay."

D.J. set down her tray on the table and slid into a plastic chair. She'd chosen to have Chinese for dinner, while Quinn had picked Italian. He offered her a slice of garlic bread.

"Not with my orange chicken," she said, "but thanks for asking."

"Anytime."

When he'd invited her to dinner, she hadn't been sure she'd wanted to accept. Nor had she wanted to say no, which made no sense but was right in line with how her life was going these days. However, if she'd tried to figure out what would happen during the dinner, she would never have imagined them dining in the middle of the food court.

"Save room for ice cream," he told her. "I'm springing for two scoops."

"Be still my heart."

He grinned. "It's the flowers, isn't it? I brought you flowers and now you're getting all gooey on me. Not that I mind."

She blinked at him. "Gooey?"

"You know. Romantic. It's nice."

She grabbed her plastic fork. "I'm not getting romantic."

"Sure you are. We can hold hands while we eat, if you'd like."

She dropped her free hand to her lap. "I don't think so."

He winked. "I like that you're shy."

Shy? If she'd been drinking she would have spit. She might be a lot of things, but shy—

She glared at him. "You're teasing me."

"Uh-huh."

She tried not to smile, but felt the corners of her mouth curve up anyway. Damn him. How did Quinn do that? All her life she'd been out of the mainstream. Never just a regular teenager or young woman. She told herself she didn't mind being different, that she had a purpose. She needed to stay safe and keep others safe. But sometimes—rarely—she wanted to be like other women her age. Carefree. Unbound by the knowledge of how deadly the world could be.

When Quinn treated her like a regular woman, she could almost bring herself to forget.

He chewed a mouthful of ziti, then swallowed. "So I was thinking about the lingerie store," he said conversationally. "After dinner, we should go back and you can model some stuff for me."

"Excuse me?"

"You're excused."

Her warm fuzzy thoughts faded. "I'm not going to prance around in sexy lingerie for you."

"Technically, I never mentioned the word *prance.* See here's the thing." He leaned forward and dropped his voice. "I've been out in the jungle for a long time, serving my country. If you were to do this, you would be, in your own personal way, aiding the defense of our nation."

She chewed her orange chicken. "Does anyone really buy into your lines?"

He winced. "That was cruel. I'm being completely honest here. You would look great in sleazy underwear. And I'm in a position to know, what with having seen you naked."

D.J. didn't know what was going on. For the past week, Quinn hadn't mentioned that night she'd gone to his hotel room. She even wondered if he'd forgotten about it. Now, suddenly, it was a topic of conversation.

"Define *sleazy,*" she told him.

He grinned. "Cut down to your belly button, up to your hipbones. Or topless. Topless works. Silk, lacy, see-through. I'm not real picky."

"I can tell."

She thought about the lingerie store they'd passed early. They carried more high-end inventory. She would describe their stock as feminine and erotic, but not sleazy. There's no way men would be allowed into the dressing room. Not that she was willing to give Quinn a fashion show for one. Still...

She remembered the bustier they'd had in the window, with some high-cut panties and a garter belt. She was too muscular to be thin, but her body had plenty of curves and definition. Some men liked that. Did Quinn?

Unhappy with the question, and with the image of herself wearing the bustier while Quinn moved ever closer, she attacked her dinner.

"I'm into cotton," she told him.

"Cotton could work. You would be hot in just about anything."

She glanced at him. Damn if the man didn't look sincere. And double damn if that sincerity didn't make her feel all warm inside. "Thanks."

"You're welcome. So you want to go back to that store?"

"Nope."

"What if I beg?"

She shook her head. "Explain the male fascination with the female body to me. I get why teenagers are interested, but once a guy hits his twenties, how can there be any mystery?"

He leaned toward her. "You're kidding, right?"

"No. I'm serious. I don't get it." She set down her fork. "During the war games, before I met up with you, there were three army officers. They were in their thirties, experienced soldiers. I sent Ronnie to circle around back while I used a frontal approach."

Quinn frowned. "You walked right up to them."

"Sort of. First I took off my shirt. I had a tank top on underneath, no bra. I twisted it and tucked it under my breasts so it was tight. Then I rolled down my pants to bikini level, loosened my hair and acted stupid. It worked perfectly.'' She took a sip of her drink. ''I'll admit that it was cold and my shirt was damp, so the breast thing should have been mildly interesting, but they were so caught up in the 'girl thing' they got caught. What's up with that?''

''I have no idea.''

''It's not as if each of them hadn't seen dozens of women's breasts before. They're *just* breasts. Why are men such saps? Can you imagine what would have happened if I'd been wearing a wet T-shirt and a thong? They would have probably told me state secrets. Frankly, anyone wearing a thong deserves that. I mean why would any rational woman want to have something tugging up her—''

D.J. noticed that Quinn's expression had glazed over. His eyes were slightly unfocused and he looked as if he was in pain.

''What?''

He made a noise low in his throat. ''Change the subject.''

''We can't talk about thongs at dinner? Why? You're the one who wanted me wearing practically nothing.''

He reached over and grabbed her chair and pulled it several inches closer. Then he took her free hand and brought it to his crotch.

D.J. dropped her fork. He wasn't just hard, he was throbbing. She felt the length and breadth of his erection but didn't understand what had caused it.

''You're turned on by thongs?'' she asked.

He groaned. ''No. By you in one. Or nothing. We have to change the subject.''

She slowly withdrew her hand. Several thoughts flooded her mind at once. They were, in no partic-

ular order, the realization that she was aroused, too.
Somehow all the talk of being naked or almost naked, of him watching, of *sex,* had left her breathless
and tingling. She also suddenly understood why
he'd been angry after they'd been intimate. He was
the kind of man who liked to share rather than just
take. He'd trusted her and she'd violated that trust.

But the overwhelming feeling she had was one of
awe. He wanted her, and he'd let her know. Even
after what had happened between them, even after
she'd refused to fully participate. Knowing she was
difficult and that admitting to desire made him vulnerable, he'd done it anyway. What she didn't know
is if he'd been afraid, or if it hadn't occurred to him
to worry.

She could slaughter him with some verbal assault,
but she didn't want to. Instead she found herself
wishing he would pull her to her feet and drag her
out to his car where he'd drive her back to his hotel
and make wild passionate love to her.

"Don't look so shocked," he said lightly. "I'll
survive."

She knew that. They would all survive. They
would get by. But somehow that didn't seem like
enough anymore.

"Quinn?"

"Don't sweat it, Daisy Jane."

Then he did the most amazing thing. He picked
up her hand and brought it to his mouth where he
pressed a soft, damp kiss against her open palm.
Desire poured through her, flooding her until she
wanted to plunge into the rising tide and never re-
surface.

The sexy, tender, erotic kiss made her want to curl

up against him. She wanted to be held, and hold him. She wanted to touch, to be naked. She wanted to feel her body pressed against him and maybe, just maybe, let herself go. Just this once.

He stared into her eyes. She felt the connection down to her soul. If he didn't want to risk asking her back to his hotel, she could invite him to her place. Except she never brought anyone home. The only person who even knew where she lived was Rebecca.

So many walls, she thought sadly. She'd been so concerned about keeping herself locked up and safe, she'd never considered who she might be keeping out.

"Ice cream?" he asked, breaking the mood and making her smile.

"Sure."

"Two scoops?"

"I always go for the gusto."

Quinn returned alone to his hotel room. He'd thought about inviting D.J. back with him, but the evening had gone so well, he hadn't wanted to risk ending it on anything but a positive note. Plus, he had a hunch she'd felt a tingle or two while they were together. Better to have her wanting. He was determined that the next time they were together, he would break through her barriers and seduce her into surrendering. In the meantime, he could tell there would be several cold showers in his future.

As he walked over to the bed, he saw the message notice on his cell phone.

He punched the number from memory, then waited for the answer.

"Banner."

Quinn heard the familiar voice of his CO. "It's Reynolds."

"There's been an unexpected development. I need a shooter. You interested?"

Quinn glanced down at the blank pad of paper. He'd been promising himself that he would make a list of the pros and cons of staying in his present job. But what was the point of that? He either wanted in or he wanted out.

If he left…then what?

He thought about Gage and Kari—their engagement, their marriage, their plans to have a house, kids, grandkids. He thought of Travis and Kyle, of Rebecca who loved her husband. Of the women like her. Could he have that?

"Quinn?"

"I'm still here." He shook his head. "No can do."

"This assignment or all of them?"

He thought of D.J. She didn't make it easy, but that was how he liked it. If he could have her…

"All of them. I want out."

His CO sighed. "You're going to be hell to replace. You've been the best."

"What does that say about me?"

"Good question. I'll need you to come in and formalize all this. No rush."

"I'll let you know when."

"Fair enough. Good luck."

"Thanks."

Quinn pushed the off button, then tossed the phone on the bed.

He'd just closed a door. Now he would wait to see what the view was like out the window.

"You reviewed the material, right?" D.J. asked, wondering why she was so edgy. She'd done this a thousand times before. Except she'd never done it with Quinn along. Could that make all the difference?

The man in question pulled the bag of supplies out of her SUV. "I looked it over several times. Relax."

"But you've never participated in this kind of a demonstration before." She led the way toward the elementary school. "I want to get it right."

He shook his head. "D.J., it'll be fine. Based on what you told me, I don't even have lines. I'm just your punching bag."

She looked at him. "We're going to be demonstrating basic self-defense for these kids. If anyone tries to abduct them, this training may be all that stands between staying safe and getting kidnapped. I take that very seriously."

"So do I."

She nodded. "I know. It's just this is important to me."

"That's why I'm here."

His steady gaze reassured her. Normally she had one of the deputies from the sheriff's office help her out, but instead of calling Travis, she'd asked Quinn.

Really stupid, she told herself. Because it smacked of finding excuses to spend time with him. Which she really hated. Life had been a whole lot easier before the war games. Back before she'd known Quinn Reynolds existed.

"You're nervous," he said, sounding surprised.

"Of course I'm nervous," she snapped as they entered the school and headed for the front office to sign in. "I'm a person, not a machine. I have emotions."

"Most of the time you try to ignore them."

She stopped in the middle of the hall and glared at him. "This is a really bad time to psychoanalyze me, okay?"

He cupped her cheek. "You'll be fine."

She practically growled. "Of course *I'll* be fine. *I'm* not the problem."

"Meaning I am?" He dropped his hand. "Not true, Daisy Jane."

"Don't call me that."

"Hmm, so if it's not me and it's not you, then what has your panties in a bunch?"

She stalked to the front desk and signed both their names. "I could kill you right now," she muttered under her breath. "I have means and motive."

"So much violence."

He waited until they were out of earshot of the secretary, then leaned close. "Someone is just a little frustrated. Or is she worried that people might think she likes a certain someone? Are you afraid the kids will see that you want me to be your boyfriend?"

She grabbed the front of his shirt. "I do *not* want you for my boyfriend," she told him, her voice loud enough to echo in the empty hallway.

D.J. instantly dropped her hand and wanted to curl up in a ball. Embarrassment heated her cheeks.

"I'll get you for this," she told him.

He chuckled. "I can't wait."

Determined to ignore him, what he said, how he made her feel and every other thing about him, she walked toward the classroom. When she reached the door, she turned back to him.

"I expect you to behave in here."

"Yes, ma'am. But if I don't, are you going to punish me when we get back to my hotel?"

She rolled her eyes, then stepped inside the room.

The teacher smiled and greeted her, as did several of the students. Most of them she'd already met. When Quinn followed her in, she introduced him to the kids, and told them why they were here.

In the middle of her explanation, she saw Quinn wink at one of the little boys. At the sight, the last of her nervousness faded and her heart gave a little squeeze.

Everything was going to be just fine.

Chapter Twelve

Quinn wasn't surprised when D.J. hopped out of the car as soon as he put it in Park. He figured her allowing him to drive in his vehicle was as much of a victory as he was going to get at one time. And it was enough.

He'd invited her to join him for a barbecue at Travis's house, and she'd accepted. Two weeks ago the mention of it would have sent her running, or put her into combat mode. She'd come a long way in a short period of time. He wondered if he was the only one who noticed, or if she'd seen the changes, too.

"Thanks for being my date," he said when he'd caught up with her.

She paused in midstep and looked at him. "Your what?"

Okay, so messing with her probably wasn't wise,

but it was too much fun. She grabbed the bait each and every time. He liked how her eyes got all bright when she was riled and how she glared at him. As if she could really take him. She was tough and determined, and underneath that facade was a heartbroken woman desperate to be held.

"My date. I asked you to join me and you accepted. What would you call it?"

"Momentary lapse of judgment," she muttered.

He ignored that. "I know you want to compliment me on how things went at the school last week. You've been trying to figure out how to tell me I was brilliant."

She rolled her eyes. "You don't actually need me here for this conversation, do you?"

"Come on. Admit it. I was good."

She sighed heavily. "Fine. You were good. You made the kids feel comfortable and that's important."

The compliment surprised him. He hadn't expected her to go along with him. "You were great, too," he told her honestly. "You're real sweet with the kids. They trust you. You're giving them information that can save them. You get them to see it's important but you don't scare them."

She turned away. "Thanks," she mumbled, and kicked at the grass. "I want to keep them safe."

"I know."

He knew more than that. He knew she worried about them, and that some of her concern came from the fact that *she'd* never felt safe herself, growing up. He wished he could change that. He would like to go back in time and make her world right.

A burst of laughter caught his attention. For the

first time he actually looked at the large house in front of them. It was a three-story Victorian on a huge lot. Half a dozen kids played in a side yard. Two young girls sat on the massive covered porch. There was a board game on the wood floor between them, and a tray with drinks and cookies.

He put his arm around D.J.'s shoulders and started forward. "Cops make more here in Glenwood than they do in Possum Landing," he said.

"I don't think so. This house, and the equally elegant homes the other Haynes siblings own are paid for by dividends from Austin's company. He's an inventor of heat-resistant polymers, or something like that. I can't remember. Anyway, they helped with the start-up money years ago and have been well rewarded for their faith. It's a great company. I bought a few shares myself."

He was pleased she hadn't pulled away from his embrace. Now he leaned close. "An amazing body, and money. You're quite the catch, Daisy Jane."

"You're the most irritating man I know."

"And yet you adore me."

She stopped at the foot of the stairs. "*Adore* is really strong. I'd be willing to admit to *tolerate*. Sometimes I tolerate you."

Coming from her, that was practically a confession of everlasting love.

"You think I'm sexy, too," he whispered, mindful of the girls on the porch.

She glanced down at the ground. "You are the most egotistical, arrogant, self-centered man—"

He silenced her with a quick kiss. She stiffened but didn't pull back. He considered that progress. When he raised his head, she looked stunned. Wanting lurked in her dark eyes, which pleased him. He'd spent the past couple of weeks in a constant state of need. There had been plenty of times when he could have ushered D.J. into his bed, but he wouldn't. Not until the moment was right. This time he wanted a very different outcome.

That condition would require her to trust him and need him. While he'd made progress on both fronts, he wanted to be sure. If they made love a second time and she was able to hold back, he knew that a pattern would have been established. The longer it went on, the more difficult it would be to break. Better to drown in cold showers than risk moving in too soon.

He took her hand and drew her up the stairs. They walked into the large house and were immediately plunged into familial chaos.

More kids ran through the front rooms. Travis and Kyle were talking, their wives at their sides. He saw Rebecca with a baby in her arms, Kari, Haley and Stephanie laughing together. Kevin and Nash shared a sofa. Family, he thought. His family.

Jordan spotted them first and called out a greeting. Suddenly Quinn and D.J. were surrounded by Hayneses, Reynoldses and Harmons. Quinn found himself shaking hands with the men and accepting hugs and kisses from the women. A couple of kids wanted to be picked up.

"Glad you two could make it," Austin said, as he put his arm around his wife. "We were wondering if you got lost."

"It was D.J.'s fault," Quinn said easily. "She takes so long with all that primping."

She shot him the death stare. "I was right on time."

As soon as the words were out, she pressed her lips together, as if she'd just realized she'd more or less implied they were together. A couple. His date, as he'd teased her earlier. Quinn waited to see if she would balk or distance herself. Instead she shrugged.

"But blaming it on the woman is so much easier, right?" she said.

He grinned. "Whatever works."

She glanced at him. The corners of her mouth quivered, then she smiled. He felt a tightness in his chest, but before he could figure out what it meant, Jill claimed D.J., then Gage walked over and the moment was gone.

"How's it going?" his brother asked him.

"Good. What about with you?"

Gage nodded at the crowd. "I hate to leave all this, but Kari and I are heading home in a few days. Kari promised to help Mom with her wedding to John, then we have to get moving on our own." Gage cuffed him lightly. "I'd like you to be my best man. Think you can swing it?"

"I'll be there."

Gage looked surprised. "Are you sure?"

Kari walked up and slipped her arm through Gage's. "Sure about what?"

"Quinn says he can make it home to be my best man."

Kari smiled at him. "I'm glad. Gage really wants you there, and I do, too. Think you can stand wearing a tux for a few hours?"

"Absolutely," Quinn told her.

"Good. Now that the family had expanded, the

guest list just got a whole lot bigger. More people means more fun, right? Oh, that reminds me, I need everyone's addresses. I better get them now before I forget.''

She kissed Gage's cheek and walked off. Gage turned and watched her go.

Quinn saw the happiness in his brother's expression. ''You look like a man in love,'' he said.

''I am.'' Gage shrugged. ''After all these years, I wasn't sure it was going to happen, but it did. She was worth the wait.''

''How'd you know she was the one?''

''I just knew. I want to tell you that it was a gradual thing. That I figured it out in stages, but that's not true. When Kari came home, I still had some feelings for her, but I didn't know if they were about the past, or what. Then I found out about Earl Haynes being our biological father and nothing was the same. That was my own personal hell, and Kari was there. I finally got that I was better with her than without her. Imagining us together in twenty or thirty years was easy. I liked what I saw in our future.''

''Sounds good.''

''It is. I want to have kids with her. I want roots.''

Quinn nodded. Roots had always been important to his brother. Gage had prided himself on being a fifth-generation Reynolds in Possum Landing. Learning that Earl Haynes was his biological father had changed everything, but he'd come through okay. Now Gage would create his own dynasty, pass on his own traditions.

''You've always known what you wanted,'' Quinn said.

Gage glanced toward D.J. "What about you? There's something going on. We can all see it."

Quinn didn't bother denying the obvious. He and D.J. *did* have something between them, but he wasn't sure what. She could be everything he'd ever wanted and needed, but what about him? Did he come close to being right for her?

"When I figure it out, I'll let you know," he said.

Travis walked over and slapped Gage on the back. "Did he tell you that he's heading back to Texas?"

"He did."

Travis shook his head. "I've done my best to talk him into staying, but he won't have any part of it."

Elizabeth joined her husband and slid her arm around his waist. "Honey, you've got to stop trying to get everyone in the family to move to Glenwood. We all think it's the perfect place to live, but Gage seems very fond of his hometown. You need to respect that."

Travis shrugged. "Can I help it if I want my brothers close?"

"I appreciate the sentiment," Gage told him. "You don't have to worry about us all losing touch. Now that we've found each other, you're stuck with us."

"I wouldn't have it any other way," Travis said.

Kyle walked up. "What about you, Quinn? You ever think about sticking around here? You could run for sheriff against Travis."

Quinn chuckled. "I don't think so. I'm not an election kind of guy."

"So challenge him to an arm wrestling match," Kyle said.

Travis shook his head. "Nope. He'd whip my butt."

"You're strong," Elizabeth told her husband.

"Quinn knows things," Travis said and kissed her. "But thanks for the support."

Quinn watched them. While he didn't begrudge them their happiness, seeing their contentment in their relationships left him feeling empty inside. As if he'd been missing out on something for a long time.

D.J. chose that moment to stroll up. She was on his side of the group, so he risked grabbing her wrist and pulling her close.

He half expected her to try to deck him. Instead she flashed him a startled glance, then stepped close enough for him to put his arm around her waist and rest his hand on her hip.

Travis and his wife looked at each other but didn't say anything. Gage grinned, as did Kyle. Quinn had a good idea about what they were all thinking. Let 'em, he told himself. No one's opinion mattered except for D.J.'s and his own.

"How long will you be staying in the military?" Elizabeth asked him. "If you don't have other plans, you could think about moving here when you get out. Even if you don't want to run for sheriff."

"Quinn always planned to stay in at least twenty years," Gage said. "That means another ten to go."

Quinn nodded. That had been his plan. Until a few days ago.

"I resigned last week."

Everyone looked surprised. Gage took a half step toward him. "What happened?"

As his brother asked the question, Quinn felt

D.J.'s hand on his back. He glanced down at her. She didn't speak, but he could read the concern in her expression. He gave her a reassuring smile, then turned his attention back to Gage.

"I wasn't willing to be that person anymore."

There was a whole lot more to it than that, but no one needed to hear the details. Later maybe he would discuss them with D.J., but not now.

Gage grinned. "Then you *will* be at my wedding."

"I said I would be."

Travis slapped him on the back. "You're welcome to stay here. Glenwood could always use another deputy."

"Or sheriff," Kyle said, then chuckled.

"I appreciate the offer. I don't know what I want to do, but when I figure it out, I'll let you know."

The conversation shifted to plans for the evening. Eventually people started drifting away. Quinn kept his arm around D.J. until they were alone, then he leaned against the wall and grabbed on to her belt loop and tugged her close.

"You've been quiet," he said.

"I'm still in shock from your bombshell. What made you change your mind?"

He shrugged. "I never liked what I did—even though I was good at it. There weren't enough rescues and there were way too many killings. That's not what I wanted."

"Makes sense."

He couldn't tell what she was thinking and it became important for him to know. Did any of this matter to her? Did she care that he was no longer going to be heading out of the country in a few weeks? Would she tell him the truth if he asked, and if she would, did he want to hear it?

"D.J...."

She cut him off with a quick shake of her head. "I'm glad," she whispered.

Two words. Two little words that hit him with the power of a rifle blast at point-blank range. The air exploded from his lungs. His chest swelled and his heart rate doubled.

"Yeah," he said, trying for cool and not sure if he made it.

He glanced around and saw a small powder room tucked under the stairs. After making sure no one was watching, he took D.J.'s hand and drew her along with him. When they'd both squeezed into the tiny room, he shut the door behind them and gathered her close.

He'd thought she might protest but instead she melted into his arms. Even as he pressed his mouth to hers, she parted for him. Tongues swept against each other. Searching, hungry, deep kisses shredded his self-control and left him desperate with wanting.

He touched her hair, her back, then dropped his hands to her rear and squeezed. She arched against him, bringing her belly in contact with his erection. She seemed as eager, as ready. Her slender fingers touched his face, then explored his chest.

"I want you," he breathed against her mouth.

He cupped her face to hold her in place, then drew back enough to nibble along her jaw. When he reached her throat, she dropped her head, exposing her soft skin. He licked the sensitive spot just behind her earlobe and made her moan. Sucking the same bit of skin made her squirm.

She wore jeans and a tank top. Quinn grabbed the straps and pulled them down her arms. The knit fabric slipped over her breasts and pinned her arms to her sides. He knew she could free herself in a second, but there was the illusion of being trapped. Not exactly D.J.'s style.

"It's all right," he whispered as he unfastened the front of her bra. "I won't hurt you. I promise."

He kissed his away down her chest to her exposed breasts. As he took one tight nipple into his mouth, he teased the other with his fingers.

She tasted sweet and hot. He was so damned hard he could have lost it right there.

"So beautiful," he told her, moving to her other breast. "Perfect curves. Your nipples are so tight." He licked the hard tip. She jumped.

"I love how you react to my touch," he said, then opened his mouth and drew her in.

He sucked rhythmically. Her breath caught, then she shifted, freeing herself of the tank top. Quinn braced himself for her rejection. But instead of pushing him away, she buried her fingers in his hair and held him in place.

"Don't stop," she whispered.

They were magic words, he thought, both relieved and gratified by her response. She trusted him. Maybe not fully, but more than he'd hoped was possible.

While he wanted to push her up onto the narrow vanity and take her right there, he knew this wasn't the time or the place. When he next made love with D.J., he wanted privacy, a big bed and a whole night. Still, a man could dream, right?

He straightened. While keeping his hands on her

breasts, he stared into her eyes and pushed his arousal against her. Her pupils dilated and her mouth parted. She shifted, parting her legs and then moving against him. Rubbing herself on his erection. Taking pleasure.

"I want you so much," he breathed. "Tell me you feel the same."

He was asking too much—he knew that. But he wanted to hear the words. *Needed* to hear them.

She pulled back a little. He kept his hands on her bare breasts.

"D.J., don't," he whispered, then kissed her.

He didn't know if he was telling her not to draw away, or giving her permission not to say the words. When she kissed him with the uninhibited passion of a woman desperate for a man, he told himself it was enough.

Eventually he became aware of his surroundings and lifted his head. "Someone's going to need this bathroom pretty damn soon," he said.

"I know."

He released her breasts and reached for her bra. "You're a terrific date."

She drew on the cotton undergarment and smiled. "You're not so bad yourself."

They both straightened their clothes. Quinn tried to adjust himself so his erection wasn't so obvious. D.J. watched, then grinned.

"You should probably stay close behind me until that goes away. Otherwise, the entire family will be talking."

"Good plan."

She reached for the door handle, then paused. "Quinn, I—" She shook her head. "I just... Hell."

She fumbled with the front of her jeans. Before he could figure out what she was doing, she unzipped them and took his hand in hers. Then she pushed his fingers down the front of her panties. He felt soft skin, softer curls, then a slick, swollen heat that made him groan.

"I do want you," she admitted, even as she turned away and fastened her jeans. "Just so you know."

Then she opened the door and stepped out into the hallway.

Stunned, aroused and more than a little awed by her courage, Quinn followed. And came face-to-face with a very amused Rebecca.

"Gee, after all this time, I would have thought you could manage the bathroom on your own," Rebecca said.

D.J. blushed. If Quinn hadn't seen it with his own eyes, he wouldn't have believed it.

"Nothing happened," D.J. told her friend.

Rebecca raised her eyebrows. "Too bad."

After the dinner, the men cleared the table, served dessert and made coffee. Quinn found himself in the kitchen, carefully cutting a large sheet cake into small pieces. Rebecca walked into the room.

"I brought you a cake server," she said as she set down a silver spatula-like device.

"Thanks."

He used it to transfer the first corner piece to a plate.

She leaned against the counter and watched Kevin pour coffee into a carafe. When he'd left, she turned her attention back to Quinn.

"I'm pleased that D.J. has finally let herself fall for someone," she told him.

Quinn was smart enough to recognize a mine field when he stepped into one. He carefully kept quiet.

Rebecca smiled. "Is the subject matter making you nervous?"

"Maybe."

"It shouldn't. You make her happy and that's good."

He scooped up another piece of cake. "Okay."

Rebecca sighed. "Fine. I'll talk. You can listen. That probably feels safer." She began putting plates on the tray. "I know there are a lot of dark secrets from D.J.'s past. Something horrible happened when she was still a kid. She doesn't talk about, but I recognize the scars."

Quinn looked at her. She shrugged.

"I've been around orphaned kids for years," she told him. "Loss and pain are fairly universal. D.J. has a wounded spirit and it's not just because her parents are dead."

"Okay."

"There's a certain irony in all of this," she continued. "D.J. has done everything she can to stay safe. At least by her definition of the word. Then she goes and falls for the one man who will always be stronger, faster, more deadly. Maybe she recognizes something of herself in you. Or maybe you see a kindred spirit."

Quinn wasn't about to go there. He still hadn't decided if normal was in the cards for him. Although if it was, he put his money on D.J. being the one.

"She doesn't trust easily," he said.

"I know, but she's starting to trust you. When

she pushes you away, and she will, take heart in that.''

He handed her a plate. ''What makes you think I'm worth it?''

''D.J. doesn't give her heart easily and never without the person earning the privilege of receiving it. Besides, I've met your brothers and I've spent time with you. You're one of the good guys.''

Yeah, right. ''Do you have any idea what I used to do for a living?''

''No. Why does that matter?''

''You wouldn't be alone with me if you had a clue.''

''You're wrong,'' she told him. ''It's not what you do, it's who you are.''

''Haven't you heard that men are what they do?''

''Sure. And you just walked away from your job. I think there's hope, Quinn Reynolds. More importantly, D.J. does.''

Rebecca was too trusting by half. ''Maybe you should warn me off. Maybe you should tell me not to hurt her.''

''I don't think you will. There's a part of me afraid she won't give you the chance. I hope she does. I hope she can open herself enough to be hurt, but I can't be sure. I wish—'' Rebecca glanced at the doorway.

D.J. walked into the kitchen. ''Don't stop talking on my account.''

''I have to. We were talking about you. It's no fun if we can't do it behind your back.'' She tried to hand D.J. the tray. ''Take this out to the dining room so we can go back to gossiping.''

"No way. I want to hear what you two were saying."

Quinn finished cutting the cake. "Not even on a bet."

D.J. moved close. "I have ways of making you talk."

Their gazes locked. Quinn felt the heat slam into his body. The wanting that always lurked just below the surface exploded to life.

Rebecca sighed. "All this sexual energy makes me want to collect my husband, take him home and have my way with him. In fact I'm going to do just that right now. 'Night all."

She walked out of the room. Quinn didn't take his gaze from D.J.'s face.

"Not a bad idea," he said.

The drive back to the hotel should have taken fifteen minutes and probably did...but to D.J. it seemed to last a lifetime. Her mind raced with a thousand questions and not a single answer. Too many things had happened in too short a period of time. Quinn's announcement that he was leaving the military. While she had a good idea why he was doing it, she didn't know why it made her feel...hopeful. His employment had nothing to do with her. Leaving the military didn't mean he was sticking around in Glenwood, nor did she want him to. He would be leaving and she wouldn't be missing him when he was gone. Really.

So why did she feel so unsettled? Was it the kiss they'd shared? The intensity of the moment had humbled her. She'd wanted with a desperation she'd never felt before. Even more startling, she'd let him know.

She felt afraid, but also alive. More alive than she'd felt in years. Fear and desire. Which would be stronger?

They pulled into the hotel parking lot. Quinn stopped the car, then turned off the engine. When he pulled the key from the ignition, he dangled it between his fingers and glanced at her.

"I want you to stay," he said quietly. "Spend the night with me, D.J."

She didn't know what to say. The word *yes* hovered on her lips, but to speak it would require a level of courage she didn't possess. Quinn didn't know what he was asking.

He touched her cheek. "Stay," he whispered. "But know this. If you walk into that hotel room with me, it has to be different. You have to be willing to trust me."

She knew what he meant. He didn't want her holding back. Honestly, she wasn't sure she could. Last time she'd barely escaped. Now that he knew what she would try to do, he would work all that much harder to make sure she surrendered. Would she be able to withstand his sensual assault? Did she want to?

She told herself that walking away was the easiest and most sensible solution. Quinn was a great guy, but did she really want to take things any further with him? Why not keep it simple?

She actually reached for the door handle, but before her fingers could close on it, her heart cried out. The sharp, painful sound ripped through her, making her ache. She'd been alone for too damn long, she thought bitterly. Alone and empty. She'd devoted her life to protecting herself, and in the end, what did she have to show for it? Yes, she was alive, but was she living? She worried about broken bones, but what about blows to her spirit? Didn't she just once want to connect with another living creature? Didn't she just once want to be like everyone else?

She looked at him, at his familiar, handsome face, at his dark eyes and the steady set of his mouth. He wanted too much, yet how could she refuse? If she walked away, would she ever have the courage to try again?

"I can't promise it will work," she told him, forcing herself to meet his gaze when all she wanted to do was duck her head.

He smiled. "Agreed. But you have to promise to try." His grin turned cocky. "I can take it from there."

She thought about how it had been the last time they'd been together and what he'd made her feel just a few hours ago in that tiny bathroom. She thought of all the times he'd understood when she'd assumed no one ever would. She thought about how she looked forward to seeing him and how much he'd come to mean to her.

Slowly she stepped out of the car. Quinn did the same. They stood on opposite sides of the vehicle. Her own SUV was just a few feet away. Easy escape, she thought. But at what price?

Then she straightened her shoulders and nodded. "Okay," she said. "I'll try."

Chapter Thirteen

D.J. was shaking when they entered Quinn's hotel room, and it wasn't from desire. The need to bolt was nearly as strong as the need to keep breathing. Every cell in her body told her this was a really, really bad idea.

When he closed the door behind them, the sound echoed in her head. Since she'd last been in here, the space had shrunk to the size of a postage stamp. There didn't seem to be anywhere to move. She couldn't catch her breath.

"Hey," he said, taking her hand and leading her to the bed. "Looking like you're going to pass out isn't doing much for my ego. I'm a guy. If you mess with my confidence, this is going to fizzle."

She tried to smile at his humor. "I don't think your ego is the problem."

He sighed. "You're right. I'm just too good."

He sat and pulled her down next to him. She wanted to bounce right back to her feet, but resisted the burning need. Instead she laced her fingers together and concentrating on slowing her increasing heart rate. Be centered, she told herself. Be relaxed. Don't throw up.

All good advice, she thought, trying to find humor in the situation. But running out that door still sounded like the best plan.

''Lie down,'' he said.

The command stunned her. She turned to him. ''What? Just like that? Should I spread my legs, too? You can do it in fifteen seconds and then I can be out of here. What a great plan.''

He ignored her tirade and slipped back onto the mattress, then patted the space next to him. ''Come on, D.J. Right here. Lie down and talk to me. That's all we're going to do. Talk.''

Gritting her teeth against the need to continue her outburst, she kicked off her shoes and did as he requested. She hated stretching out next to him. She felt awkward and ungainly. All arms and legs, with nowhere to put them.

Quinn propped his head up on one hand and rested the other on her stomach. She jumped at the contact, then tried to slow her breathing.

''What?'' she demanded, sounding more curt than she'd planned.

He didn't speak. Instead he slowly rubbed her belly. Around and around. Like she was some damn cat, she thought resentfully.

''Have you ever allowed yourself to climax while making love?''

That sure cut to the heart of the matter, she

thought suddenly embarrassed. She closed her eyes and shook her head.

"Ever get close?"

Could they please stop talking and just do it? Except she couldn't say that and she still couldn't look at him, so she nodded.

"Sometimes," she whispered. "Not often. If I get too...interested, it's pretty easy to change direction."

"When you and I were together, I thought you were close," he said. "Was I right?"

She nodded. "It would have been easy to, um, you know."

"So none of this is about my abilities in bed."

She opened her eyes and glared at him. "Do you have to make everything about yourself?"

"Pretty much." He continued to rub her stomach. "It's okay that you're nervous. And scared. I understand that. All I want from you is the promise that you'll be open to the experience. Just lie there and let me seduce you."

He leaned close. "I'm going to touch you all over." He bent down and kissed her neck. "With my fingers, my lips and my tongue."

He demonstrated by lightly licking her skin. Instantly goose bumps erupted and her breasts began to swell. Anticipation grew, slowly pushing out the fear.

"I'm going to take off all your clothes," he continued. "When you're naked, I'm going to look at you because you're so beautiful. Then I'm going to work my way up from your toes. When I get here..." He moved his hands from her belly to that place between her legs. "I'm going to touch you and taste you and pleasure you until neither of us can stand it. All you have to do is lie back and let me.''

D.J. suddenly felt as if she were on fire. Her arms and legs felt heavy. Her brain wasn't working as quickly as usual, and she was already wet and swollen.

In the past she'd never allowed a man to do what Quinn was talking about. Everything about it made her feel too vulnerable. But suddenly she wanted to know what it would be like to experience that most intimate kiss. She wanted to feel his hot breath, his firm lips, his searching tongue.

She had to swallow before she could speak. "If I don't like it, will you stop?"

"Of course." He returned his hand to her belly. "You don't have to say yes, D.J. All you have to do is not say no. I'm going to wait for a count of three. If you remain silent, I'm going to start seducing you. Fair enough?"

She wanted. For the first time in her life, the need was greater than the fear. In fact she couldn't even find the fear anymore. She was hot and wet and shivering with anticipation. She needed him desperately. A small corner of her brain whispered that maybe she needed to trust more than she needed to experience sexual release, but she would wrestle with that issue another time. Right now she wanted to live the erotic image Quinn had planted in her brain. She wanted to lose herself in his arms and know what it was like to surrender to a man. To this man.

"One," he said slowly, his gaze steady on her face, his mouth curved slightly. "Two."

She reached up and wrapped her arms around his neck, then drew him close.

"Three," she whispered.

They met in an openmouthed kiss that sent her senses flying into the stratosphere. Liquid heat poured through her, making her ache and need with an intensity that took her breath away. His tongue swept inside her mouth, touching hers, teasing, tasting, taking and offering in a sensual combination that made her whimper.

He touched her back, her hips, her rear. He stretched out next to her, pulling her close, so she could feel him as well. The length of his legs, the breadth of his chest, the hardness of him.

He wanted her. If the fear returned, she would hang on to that one thought. He wanted her. He'd told her and shown her and his presence here, in this bed, reminded her this was important to him. He was willing to work much harder than most men she'd met. While she wanted to know why, she didn't ask the question. Not only because the answer would terrify her, but because she didn't want him to stop kissing her. Not now and maybe not ever.

His mouth still pressed against her, he shifted so he straddled her. His fingers tangled in her long braid, then slowly began to pull the strands free. When her hair was loose, he buried his hands in it and rubbed her scalp. Then he straightened and drew her tank top up and over her arms.

When he'd tossed the garment aside, he bent down and kissed her chin, then her jaw. He nibbled her earlobe, licked her neck and slowly moved down her chest to the edge of her plain, cotton bra.

His fingers made short work of the hook in front.

She felt cool air on her bare breasts, then his warm mouth settled on her left breast. His hand covered the right. Fingers and thumb teased her taut, sensitive nipple as his tongue matched the movements. Wanting poured through her. She reached for him, then let her hands fall back onto the bedspread as heat and passion made it impossible to move.

She could barely breathe. There was only the moment and the sensations. The tugging of her nipples, the ribbons of desire weaving through her pliant body. Quinn had talked of surrender. Right now she couldn't imagine anything else.

He shifted to one side and reached for the fastening of her jeans. When he'd lowered the zipper, he moved to the end of the bed and tugged them off. Her panties went along for the ride and when he knelt between her ankles, she was naked.

A vague uneasiness settled over her. This was the place she usually took control of the sexual encounter. Often she would shift the man onto his back, reach for the condom and make sure he didn't have a rational thought in his brain until he was finished.

Old habits died hard. But even as a part of her brain told her to sit up and get Quinn on his back, the rest of her remembered the promise to try. To let him seduce her. To let go…just this once.

The concept was foreign, but not so difficult to comprehend. Not when he lightly bit her ankle and made her giggle. He nibbled his way up her calf, then sucked on her knee.

"What are you doing?" she asked with a laugh. "That tickles."

She squirmed, but he didn't release her. Instead

he transferred his attentions to her other knee and sucked on it. She writhed.

"I don't want to kick you in the teeth," she told him.

He raised his head and smiled. "An excellent philosophy I would encourage."

Then he ducked back down. But instead of returning to her knees, he began to work his way up her thighs.

He'd been more than clear about his destination, and his intent. She was nervous, apprehensive and more than a little excited by what he planned to do. Rebecca had talked about Austin doing that to her once. Her friend's dreamy expression had made D.J. feel more than a little left out. In truth, men had offered, but she'd never been willing to let them be that intimate.

Still, as Quinn kissed and licked and nibbled his way closer, she couldn't seem to keep her legs together. They fell open of their own accord and when she felt his hot breath on her waiting dampness, she didn't pull away.

"So beautiful," he murmured as he slipped his fingers into her swollen flesh.

A shiver rippled through her. The heat grew and for the first time she became aware of a rising tension. Her muscles quivered and contracted, her blood raced, and every part of her body focused on that one feminine place.

He reached for her hands, drawing them between her thighs and urging her to part for him. Despite the promise of pleasure, she felt exposed and vulnerable. Still, she'd said she would try, so she braced herself for the assault.

But instead of kissing her *there,* he nipped on one of her knuckles. She jumped and opened her eyes.

''What do you think you're doing?'' she asked.

''Trying to keep things from being too serious.'' He sat up. ''Pull your knees back.''

She swallowed, then did as he asked, drawing her knees up and away, exposing herself even more.

''How are you doing?'' he asked. ''Nervous?''

He wanted to *talk* about it? ''Do we have to have this conversation or can we just get to it?'' she asked between gritted teeth.

''That's my girl,'' he said, and grinned. ''Ever the delicate flower. It, D.J.? This isn't 'it.' We're making love.''

Then, while she was still in shock from what he'd said, he lay back down on the bed and pressed his mouth against her.

She'd fought against that particular intimacy ever since she'd surrendered her virginity to Bobby McNare in her senior year of high school. As Quinn's tongue gently stroked her most sensitive spot and pleasure swept through her, she couldn't help wondering why.

He kissed her with a softness that left her breathless and needing. He moved over and around, sometimes fast, sometimes slow. She felt her control slipping as the need grew. Her body rebelled, wanting, striving. Tension spiraled to unbearable levels, settled there, then moved higher. Her muscles tightened. Her heels dug into the mattress. She parted her legs more, drew back her knees and pressed against Quinn's mouth.

More. She needed more. More of the slow licks, the leisurely explorations. When he lightly sucked on that one spot, she actually groaned. There was no doubting her body's destination, and if she was to pull back, this was the time. Maybe the last time.

But it felt too good. She didn't want him to stop. She didn't want to be swollen and frustrated. Just this once she wanted to let herself go. Just this once. Just with Quinn.

He loved her with his mouth. She knew now that this wasn't just sex. Not in the way she'd known it in the past. This was so much more. A man who actually cared about her and her response. A man who understood her in ways no one ever had before. She wanted to show him that his faith in her hadn't been misplaced, that she was worthy of his attentions. That—

He inserted a finger inside of her. Slowly, deeply, then pulled it out again. At the same time, he stroked her faster and faster. The combination of actions was too much. One second she was standing on the edge and the next…she fell.

Her climax caught her by surprise. Her entire body convulsed into mindless pleasure as powerful muscles contracted over and over. She cried out and shook and begged and still the waves of blissful release swept through her. It went on and on until the shudders slowed.

When she was finally still, she opened her eyes. He raised his head and looked at her. The fear returned, a cool trickling sensation that warned her she was in mortal danger. But Quinn didn't attack. Instead he kissed her palm, then shifted so he was kneeling between her legs, and smiled.

"Am I good in bed or what?" he asked.

If he'd said something emotionally significant,

she might have bolted for the door. If he'd mocked her, she would have tried to kill him. Instead he made it all about himself, and made her laugh at the same time.

She grinned. "You're okay."

"Just okay? I would have thought I deserved at least a 'very good' for that performance."

"You were okay."

His smile faded and he lightly touched her knee. "Are you going to freak out on me?"

She might have a second ago, but now she felt fine. "Not unless you morph into an alien."

"That wasn't my plan. Instead I thought I'd rip my clothes off and have my way with you."

"That works."

While he undressed, she rose and walked into the bathroom where she found the box of condoms in his shaving kit and took one out. Before she turned to leave, she glanced at herself in the mirror.

She looked like a woman who had been well pleasured. Her hair was tousled, her mouth swollen, her skin flushed. She was naked and content. And happy.

The last surprised her the most. She wasn't afraid; she didn't want to run. Instead she wanted to feel Quinn inside of her, filling her, taking his pleasure in her. She wanted to be with him, bodies touching, straining. She wanted him.

Caught up in the delight of that thought, she turned and returned to the bedroom.

Quinn was on the bed. He'd stripped off his clothes and lay on his side, his arousal jutting out toward her. She tossed him the condom and slid onto the mattress.

"Take me, big boy. I'm all yours."

Her light, teasing voice touched him down to his heart. Quinn had been surprised and pleased by D.J.'s acceptance of their lovemaking, and thrilled when she'd allowed herself to climax, but it was her acceptance after the fact that gave him the most pleasure. She wasn't second-guessing herself or them. She wasn't pulling back. Somehow she'd decided to trust him, and there was no way he would do anything to violate that trust.

He slipped on the protection, then moved close and kissed her. When her breathing had increased and her hands roamed over his body with an eagerness that made control nearly impossible, he pushed her onto her back and knelt between her legs.

Eyes locked on hers, he moved into her waiting dampness. She stretched to accommodate him, then caught her breath as he slipped back out. Her mouth opened in a soundless gasp.

"What was that?" she asked, then grabbed him by his hips and pulled him in.

This time as he filled her, he felt a faint ripple. A tightness that sucked him in deeper. She arched toward him, her fingers digging into his rear.

"More," she gasped.

He plunged in again and again. Each time he felt the same tightening as her body shuddered. The faster he moved, the more she demanded. She wrapped her legs around him and drew him in deeper.

She was strong and powerful, yet the most feminine woman he'd ever known. Her surrender humbled him, even as the rippling contractions worked on his self-control until it shattered and he couldn't hold back anymore.

"I can't wait," he gasped.

Her eyes opened. "I don't want you to," she whispered and pulled him in deeper still.

He lost himself in the pleasure of his explosive release. As he did, he felt her body shudder and contract. She sucked in a breath, then screamed as she lost herself in release after release. Their gazes locked, their rapid breathing synchronized, he watched her face, her eyes, and saw down to the perfection of her soul.

D.J. awoke with the feeling that she couldn't breathe. The tightness in her chest propelled her into a sitting position. She recognized the symptoms immediately, but telling herself it was a panic attack didn't keep her from feeling that she was going to die.

She sat up and consciously fought her rising terror. As the covers fell away, she realized she was naked, and with that realization the events of the evening flashed through her mind. Suddenly the panic attack made sense.

Slowly, carefully, so as not to disturb Quinn, she crawled out of bed and made her way to the bathroom. When she'd shut the door behind her, she bent over at the waist and struggled to breathe. Determination battled the fight-or-flight response and slowly her rational side began to win. When the tightness faded and the panic was more manageable, she straightened and turned on the sink tap.

After washing her face with cool water, she grabbed a towel. The small nightlight illuminated her naked body. Not wanting to see that or think about what had happened, D.J. turned away from her reflection. But instead of returning to the bed-room, she leaned against the counter and fingered the white towel.

Last night…last night had been amazing, she thought. Terrifying and wonderful and awe-inspiring and horrible and life changing. Quinn confused her. He was so tender and caring, yet the man killed for a living. At least he had. How could he have lived through all that and still have a soul? How could he be so tender with her? How could he understand her?

She sucked in a breath. That's what got her the most. He *knew*. Somehow he'd figured out her fear and he'd worked to overcome it. Why? Shouldn't he be only interested in himself and his own plea-sure? Why had he taken the time and made the ef-fort. Why—

Her breath caught as an unexpected sob ripped through her. Even as tears filled her eyes and spilled down her cheeks, D.J. couldn't figure out what was going on. There was a second sob, then a third. She grabbed the towel and pressed her face into it to muffle the sound. What was wrong with her? She never cried. Never.

But this time she couldn't stop. The tears poured down her face as her body shook. Harsh, deep, pain-ful cries tore at her throat. She didn't know why she was crying or why she couldn't stop. Her whole body ached, from the inside out. She felt as if she were being ripped into a million pieces.

The bathroom door opened, and Quinn stepped into the small space. Humiliation made her turn away. But there was nowhere to run. Not that he would have let her.

Instead he put his hands on her shoulders and turned her to him. He pulled the towel away and wrapped his arms around her body. As the sobs continued to choke her, he smoothed her hair and murmured softly. Not words, just comforting sounds.

Not knowing what else to do, she clung to him. He was warm and strong and safe in a spinning world she no longer recognized. The soft brush of his mouth on her forehead was comforting, although she couldn't say why. The steady beat of his heart calmed her. She cried and cried until she was nothing but a hollow shell, and still he held her.

Some time later, perhaps just a few minutes, perhaps as much as an hour, the crying slowed. D.J. was still unsure of what was wrong with her, but she had a feeling it was related to her sexual encounter with Quinn. Had her body's release somehow affected other parts of her being?

He continued to stroke her bare back. His large hands moved slowly along her skin. Suddenly the contact wasn't as comforting as it had been. She became aware of their nakedness, of his maleness pushed up against her belly, of her bare breasts flattening against his chest. Liquid heat filled her, then settled between her thighs. Her nipples got tight, her breathing increased.

Quinn didn't seem to notice. He continued to hold her with a tenderness that made her ache. But when she reached for one of his hands and brought it to her bare breast, the response was immediate.

He went from resting to ready in less than five seconds. She shifted so that she could sit on the edge of the counter, then parted her legs. He groaned.

After fumbling in his shaving kit, he pulled out a condom and hastily tore the package open.

As he slipped on the protection, she kissed and nipped at his chest. She flicked her tongue over his nipples and smiled when they hardened and he shuddered. Then he was pushing in her and she couldn't think anymore, she could only feel.

Feel his hardness filling her. Feel the pressure building as he slid in and out. She wrapped her legs around him, pulling him close. He cupped her rear and drew her closer still. He pumped in and out, and with each aggressive thrust, she got closer and closer until all she had to do was keep breathing. The fall was inevitable.

Her first climax crashed over her like a hot wave of pleasure. The second was better and the third made her scream. Again and again, until she couldn't breathe, until he finally called out in guttural release. Until they were still.

The tears returned. Not the sobs, just silent tears spilling down her cheeks. She could no more explain them than stop them. But Quinn didn't ask. Instead, after tossing the condom into the trash, he gathered her close, picked her up and carried her into the bedroom.

When they were both under the covers, he simply held her close and lightly kissed her. She clung to him, even after the tears had faded. And when he told her to go to sleep, she closed her eyes and did what he'd requested.

D.J. woke with the sun in her eyes. She turned over and was stunned to find it was after nine. She *never* slept in—not even when she was sick. Even more shocking was the sight of Quinn up, showered, dressed and reading the paper. He'd done all that and she hadn't heard him?

"Morning," he said when he glanced up from the newspaper and saw her looking at him. "I ordered breakfast. It should be here in a few minutes, if you want to head into the bathroom first."

She blinked. "You made a phone call?"

"Yeah. I've tried placing orders using my powers of mental telepathy, but they usually get them wrong."

He looked exactly as he had the previous day. There was nothing different about his teasing, his smile, his dark eyes.

She braced herself for questions, but there didn't seem to be any. Was it possible he just accepted what had happened between them as normal? Didn't he want to talk about it?

"You probably have time for a shower," he continued. "There's shampoo by the tub. None of that girly stuff, though. This is macho shampoo."

She guessed the answer to her question was no. He didn't see the need. Which both pleased and terrified her.

She didn't want to get up and walk past him, what with being naked and all, but she really had to go to the bathroom. So she threw back the covers and stood up. As she walked by Quinn, he reached out and took her hand. He kissed her palm, then smiled at her.

"Thank you," he said.

That was all. Just thanks.

Her chest got tight, but not in a panic-attack sort

of way. Her heartbeat got weird, too, and her skin felt all prickly. She bent down and hugged him.

"Quinn, I—"

But then she didn't know what to say. He stroked her cheek.

"I know, Daisy Jane. Me, too. Now go take your shower."

She straightened and headed for the bathroom. While she had no idea what she'd been saying, or what he'd agreed with, she felt happy and giddy and light enough to fly. She didn't even have to look out the window and check the weather to know it was going to be a very good day.

Chapter Fourteen

"We had sex," D.J. said as she paced the length of Rebecca's kitchen.

Her friend smiled at her. "How was it? I would think that Quinn's finely honed hunter instincts would play very nicely in the bedroom."

D.J. glared at Rebecca. "This isn't funny. We're talking about my life here."

"If we can't find humor in our lives, what's left?"

D.J. shook her head. "I know. I'm being completely horrible and irrational, but if you knew what had happened. I mean what *really* happened." She stopped and pressed her lips together.

She didn't want to say anymore. There was no way she could confess the truth about *everything*. Not even to her best friend. But without some details, Rebecca wouldn't get how terrible everything was. How out of sorts she, D.J., felt.

She sucked in a breath and braced herself. "I cried."

Rebecca sat at the kitchen table and sipped her morning coffee. When she heard D.J.'s confession, she merely set down her mug and said, "Oh?"

D.J. stomped her foot. "'Oh?' That's it? I cried. Me. The emotionless one. The fighter. The brave, brash, fearless one. I sobbed my heart out and then we had sex right there on the bathroom counter."

"What I really want to know is, wasn't it cold to sit on tile, but I won't ask. I can see that wasn't your point."

D.J. felt like screaming. "You're not taking this seriously."

"I know, and I'm sorry. It's just that I can't figure out what the big deal is. We all cry."

"Not me. Not ever. And certainly not in front of some guy."

Rebecca rose and crossed to stand in front of her. "Quinn isn't 'some guy.' He's special. You care about him. You trust him. You're in love with him." She sighed. "Finally. I'd wondered if you would ever find the right one and you have. I think it's wonderful."

D.J.'s mind froze. Five words repeated themselves over and over in her sluggish brain as the icy cold seeped into her body.

You're in love with him.

In love? With a man? With the enemy?

"No way. Not now, not ever."

Rebecca shrugged. "Sorry. Even you don't get to

pick and choose when it comes to matters of the heart.''

Panic threatened, which was the last thing she needed. She already felt more fragile than a china doll. ''I can't.''

''You do. And for what it's worth, I think you picked a great guy. Quinn is the right match for you. He's tough enough that you won't be able to walk all over him, but he's also tender and caring. You two have a lot in common. In fact, he's perfect. For you, I mean.''

D.J. felt as if she'd been gut shot. She pressed a hand against her stomach and took an unsteady step back. Love?

''No,'' she said, and grabbed her keys. ''I have to go.''

''Wait,'' Rebecca called. ''Don't be afraid. He's not going to hurt you. D.J.!''

D.J. was already running toward her SUV. When she reached it, she ducked inside and quickly started the engine. Love? No. She would never risk it. She couldn't. Not with a man like Quinn—a man who was faster, stronger and five times more deadly.

D.J. swung her foot out and connected with Quinn's arm. He was surprised by the force in the blow, but didn't say anything. She'd been edgy ever since he'd shown up for their practice, and after what they'd shared two nights ago, he couldn't blame her. He, too, was still trying to adjust to what had happened.

He'd set out to seduce her and he'd had high hopes for a night of hot sex. What he hadn't expected was the intimacy of sharing that with her.

They'd connected on a level he'd never experienced before. If he was still putting all the pieces together, it made sense that D.J. was having the same problem.

She'd stayed for breakfast the previous morning and then had left. He hadn't seen her since. Last night he'd wondered if he should go talk to her, but he'd wanted to give her time. So he'd waited until their scheduled session this morning to see her.

She shifted her weight and kicked out again. This time he sidestepped the attack and she tumbled onto the mats. He bent over and offered his hand. She ignored the gesture, climbing to her feet by herself.

Typical, he thought, more amused than annoyed. When in doubt, retreat. It was a tactic he used himself, although he'd never had a chance to in matters of the heart. He'd never cared before. Still, with D.J.'s fears and her past, he understood her need to be wary. He understood a whole lot more than she knew. He'd even understood her tears.

They had touched him more than anything. More than her willingness to enjoy making love, more than her pleasure and the way she'd lost herself to passion. Her tears had been a reaction to years of holding herself apart. They'd exposed the vulnerability of her heart. He'd held her because he'd needed to be close as much as she had. All these years he'd wondered if he would find someone who could understand and accept him. He didn't care that she'd turned out to be prickly, difficult and scarred. He was scarred, too. They could heal together.

She circled around him and faked another kick, then punched with her right arm. The blow connected with his midsection. She might be a woman and at a disadvantage when it came to upper-body strength, but she punched like a guy.

As the air rushed out of his lungs, he took a step back. D.J. moved in closer and punched again. This time he batted her arm around. She turned and kicked.

During practice sessions she was always focused and determined. She never quit, never slacked off. But this was different. He had the feeling she was out for blood.

"We're done," he said, stepping off the mat.

"What? Why are you stopping? We're not through."

"I am."

He crossed to the small refrigerator and pulled out a bottle of water. Her reaction shouldn't surprise him. After what they'd shared, he'd thought she would back off. But not this much. He couldn't help being disappointed.

"It's because I'm getting good, isn't it?" she taunted. "You can't stand that."

He glanced at her. She stood in the center of the mats, her hands on her hips. He recognized the symptoms. She was flushed, bouncing with energy and ready for a fight.

"You're not here for a lesson," he said. "You're here because you're angry. Probably more with yourself than me, but I'm the easier target."

"I didn't realize you had a degree in psychology," she sneered. "Thanks for the analysis. So you're a gentleman killer. How new century."

He unscrewed the top on the water bottle and took a long drink. The action gave him time to access the damage her emotional hit had inflicted. Because after all this time, she knew exactly where to send in the warhead.

He was a killer. He could cover the truth with fancy words and patriotic stories, but that was the truth he couldn't escape.

"I'm out of here," he said, heading for the door.

"Because you can't stay to fight? What's the problem, Quinn? Afraid? But I'm just a girl. I can't be that much of a challenge for a professional like you. Come on, big guy. You can take me."

He stopped and faced her. "Why are you doing this? We had something amazing, D.J. Why do you want to destroy it?"

She walked toward him. "What I want to do is kick your butt. I want to beat you. I want to make you admit that I'm better."

She wasn't. She couldn't be, and they both knew it. So what the hell was going on?

Before he could decide what to do, she came at him. He shifted and batted away her kick. She tried to punch him. He put up his arm to block her just as she dropped her hands, and he accidentally came within inches of hitting her in the face.

Instantly he swore and stepped back. "What the hell was that?" he asked, feeling set up. "What are you playing at?" She'd deliberately faked him out, but why? So he would hurt her?

"Hit me," she yelled. "You know you want to." She rose on her toes and leaned toward him. "Do it."

He couldn't have been more horrified if she'd shot him. He swore silently and took another step back. Whatever this game was, he didn't want a part of it.

"Hit me!" she screamed.

And then he knew. All of it. The fury, the fear, the need to lash out and why he had to be the enemy. With the knowledge came sadness and a sense of loss. Both were bitter and metallic on his tongue, like blood.

He'd thought, he'd hoped…but he'd been wrong.

"I'm sorry," he told her, his voice quiet.

She practically vibrated with rage. "Don't be sorry, you bastard. Just do it!"

He shook his head. "I can't. I won't. But all of this—" He motioned to her, then to the room. "It's my fault. I thought if you saw what we could be like together, that it would be enough. But it's not. I can't fight your ghosts, D.J. And you won't."

"What the hell are you babbling about?"

"You. Us. Night before last we connected in a way that shook both of us."

She rolled her eyes. "In your dreams."

He ignored her. "I'm scared, too, but the difference is, I don't want to walk away from it. I'm willing to say that you matter to me. That *we* matter. That there's something special here."

"There's nothing here," she yelled. "Nothing."

"You're right," he said. "My mistake."

He reached out and took her hand in his. She tried to twist away, but he wouldn't let her. Still he was careful not to hurt her.

"You want me to hit you," he said, "because if I do, you can walk away. If I hit you, then I'm just like the rest of them, and you're right. You don't have to care."

He released her. "I'm going to make it easy on you, D.J. I'm not going to make you face your demons. I'm going to leave."

"Coward."

He shook his head. "Funny how all this time I worried about being good enough for you. I never saw you weren't good enough for me."

She went white but didn't speak.

He shrugged. Only a fool would expect more.

He started for the door, then paused and glanced back at her. "I haven't been in a fight since I was fifteen, and I sure as hell never hit a woman. But you already know that. You know I would never hurt you. But that doesn't matter because you made up your mind not to trust me before we even met. You won't trust anyone, and I'm the worst of the bunch. I'm faster, stronger and better trained, and you aren't willing to risk that."

"You have no right to judge me," she told him, her eyes narrowed, her mouth set. "You didn't live my life."

"You're not that eleven-year-old little girl anymore. Can't you see that?" He wondered why he was bothering. She wouldn't listen. But for reasons that weren't clear, he couldn't stop trying.

"You live your life in a emotional plastic bubble," he said. "No one gets in and you don't get hurt. But is that a life? Is that what you want? I'm willing to walk away from what I've known and start over. Why aren't you? I thought we could matter to each other. I thought we were each other's perfect match. But you don't want an equal. You want someone you can push around. You've lived in fear your entire life, avoiding men like your father. Well, guess what, D.J.? You haven't avoided him enough. You've turned into him. You're only interested in people you can bully, just like him."

* * *

D.J. watched him walk away. She couldn't speak, couldn't go after him, couldn't even breathe. Instead she sank to her knees as the blows that were his words attacked her. She felt ripped apart, exposed and left for dead. She curled up on the floor, pulling her knees to her chest and trying not to let the pain overwhelm her.

He was wrong, she told herself as she squeezed her eyes shut. He was wrong. About all of it. Most especially about her.

But there were too many fragments of truth for her to ignore. Too many whispers that he might be right. Too much shame for her to turn her back. Quinn had held a mirror up to her psyche, and she was stunned to find someone she hated staring back at her.

"My father used to beat me and my mother," D.J. said tonelessly, and recounted the story of her broken arm and the trip to the hospital. She spoke of how her mother had sent her to school the next day, then had killed her husband and herself.

Rebecca listened quietly. When D.J. finished, she shifted on the sofa so she could touch D.J.'s hand.

"I'm sorry," she murmured.

D.J. nodded. "But not surprised."

Rebecca shrugged. "You have scars. I've worked with enough wounded kids to have had an idea about how you got them." She leaned back into the cushions. "I don't understand people like that. People who abuse and abandon their children. What makes them do it? Why can't they see how sick they are and get help? And how dare your mother choose

death over staying with you? She could have run.''
She frowned. ''This kind of information makes me
furious.''

''Thanks for caring about me. It means a lot.''

More than a lot, D.J. told herself. It meant everything.

She glanced around at her small living room—the
place she'd once thought of as a sanctuary. Now it
was little more than the place she paced the nights
away. It was cold and dark, even with the sun shin-
ing. She had thought if she confessed the truth to
her friend, she would find peace. But her heart still
ached, and she knew she would never be warm
again.

''I was wrong,'' she whispered, fighting back
tears. ''I was wrong not to trust him. I was scared
so I lashed out.''

''You made a mistake. We all do. For what it's
worth, Quinn was wrong, too.'' Rebecca smiled.
''You're not a bully, D.J. You never were.''

''I'm exactly like my father. I only want to be
around people I can control.''

Rebecca laughed. ''Give me a break. In this
friendship, I'm the strong one, not you.''

D.J. nearly fell over in shock. ''What are you saying? You're a…a…girl.''

''I'm a woman who is content with her life and
her place in the world. There isn't anyone more
powerful than that.''

D.J. understood. Rebecca lived her life out of love
and hope, while D.J. existed in fear.

She'd spent the past week looking at herself and
seeing ugly truths. She'd discovered the dark corners

of her soul, and what she found there made her shudder.

"I don't know how to be different," she whispered.

"Yes, you do. You're already changing." She winked. "Daisy Jane."

"I can't believe I told you that."

"I'm impressed. And I can see why you go by your initials."

D.J. smiled. "Thanks for being so supportive."

"I want to do whatever I can to help, but this isn't about me, is it? It's about Quinn."

D.J. didn't want to think about him. It hurt too much. "He was right there. He said he cared about me. He showed it in everything he did. And I tossed it all back in his face."

Her eyes burned. She started to blink back the tears, only to remember that she was done hiding behind a facade. She was going to be who she really was, even if that meant facing her demons head-on. She wasn't going to run anymore.

"I said some horrible things," she murmured as she brushed away the tears. "He'll never forgive me."

He'd probably already forgotten about her. It had been a week. Each day she'd wondered if he would get in touch with her. If he would try to make things right. But he hadn't. No doubt he didn't think she was worth the trouble. She couldn't blame him. He'd talked about finding a match. His match would be someone whole and loving. Not someone like her.

She shrugged. "I'll get over him."

"I guess that means you're not willing to admit you love him."

It had taken D.J. three days to be able to admit the truth to herself. Now she was about to admit it to someone else. Talk about scary.

She looked at her friend. "I *do* love him. I know that means the whole 'getting over' part is going to take a lot longer." A lifetime. "He's the best thing that ever happened to me, and I let him get away."

"You sure did. Bummer. So you figure he's long gone, right?"

"Yeah. I thought about getting in touch with Gage and asking him where Quinn went, but—" she swallowed "—I'm too scared."

"You know Gage is back in Texas, right?"

"Uh-huh. Travis told me."

Rebecca studied her nails. "Gage left with Kari, and Kevin and Haley are gone, too. Nash is staying, of course. You'd think Quinn would have blown this Popsicle stand, yet he's still camped out at his hotel. I wonder why."

D.J.'s heart stood still. Hope filled her. It was scary and unfamiliar, but it was a whole lot better than loss and pain. She stood. "He's here? He's in town?"

"Yup. What do you suppose that means?"

D.J. pulled Rebecca to her feet, then hugged her close. "It means I have a chance. Doesn't it?"

Rebecca straightened and smiled. "I think it means you have a really good one. But a word of advice." She fingered D.J.'s stained T-shirt. "You haven't showered in days. You might want to take a second to clean up before you go try to win back your man. And wear something sexy. Guys like that.''

Two hours later D.J. studied herself in the full-length mirror on her closet door. As much as she'd wanted to rush right over to Quinn's hotel room, she'd taken Rebecca's advice and showered. Then she'd agonized over what to wear. Now she was ready to leave and not sure if she had the courage to go.

Could she face Quinn and apologize for what she'd done and said? When she thought about some of the things she'd told him, she wanted to hide in a closet for the next twenty years. Except she'd spent the past sixteen years hiding—from her past, from what she was afraid of, from what she'd become. As Quinn had pointed out, she'd cut herself off from life. It was time to change everything.

Quinn was her world. She loved him. If she wanted a chance to prove that, she was going to have to start by seeing him.

She gave herself a once-over and wished she'd asked Rebecca to stay. She wanted another opinion. Did she look sexy or just stupid? Did it matter? She wanted Quinn, and if he wanted her, he was going to have to realize she didn't do the girl thing very well. But she was willing to learn. Not necessarily for him, but also for herself. She needed to explore the side of herself she'd been denying for so long. But first she had to figure out if Quinn was willing to give her a second chance.

Quinn tossed his T-shirts in the suitcase. He'd waited a week because he'd hoped D.J. would come around and see things as they were. She'd hadn't and there was no other reason to stay in Glenwood.

Travis had tried to convince him to take a job at the sheriff's office. While Quinn intended to join the mainstream, he couldn't do it here. Not with D.J. so close. Knowing she was in the same town, walking the same streets, seeing the same people—it would hurt too much. He'd finally found the one woman he could be with and she wasn't interested. Life had a hell of a sense of humor.

He crossed to the bathroom and collected his shaving kit. There was still an unopened box of condoms tucked inside. When he'd first met D.J. and had realized how much she turned him on, he'd practically bought out the drugstore's supply of protection. Optimistic bastard, he thought grimly. Now she was out of his life and all he had was—

A knock at the door made him turn. He dropped the box back into his shaving kit and walked into the bedroom. There was a second knock.

"Coming," he called and reached for the door handle. When he pulled the door open, he started to speak, then found he couldn't.

D.J. stood in the hallway. At least he was pretty sure it was her. His eyes saw and his brain registered, but neither body part believed.

She wore a black leather minidress, high heels and nothing else that he could see. Based on how high the hem came and how low the front dipped, he doubted there *was* anything else. Full, soft curls tumbled down her back. Makeup accentuated wide, frightened eyes. She was gorgeous. A sexual goddess. If she'd come here to seduce him, he was going to have a tough time telling her no.

She opened her mouth, then closed it. After shaking her head, she pushed past him and entered the room.

"I was wrong," she said, talking quickly. "About everything. You, me, my past. I was an idiot. Worse, I hurt you. I said horrible things and I'm sorry."

He closed the door. Both wary and intrigued, he folded his arms over his chest. "Go on."

"I shouldn't have taunted you that day," she said, her voice low. She swallowed. "I was scared and angry. What we'd done, what I'd felt—it terrified me. You were right about me living in an emotional plastic bubble. I kept the world at bay because caring to me was the same as dying. What I didn't see was that living alone was a different kind of death."

She laced her fingers together in front of her stomach. "You've been so patient with me and I don't know why. I mean, why did you bother? Why didn't you just walk away?"

"There aren't many out there like you," he told her. "You're tough and vulnerable. Feminine, strong and hell on wheels. How could I resist?"

Some of the fear faded from her eyes. "Really? I thought maybe it was because I don't mind about your past. I understand what you've done and I'm okay with it. You're a good man. The best. What you did doesn't change that. I know you're stronger than me, and better and faster and all those things and it's okay. You'll never hurt me."

At her words, the tightness around his chest eased. He drew in a deep breath and moved close. They were so right for each other, he thought contentedly. She'd finally seen that.

"What are you saying, Daisy Jane?"

"That I agree with what you told me last week. That we're a match."

"I was telling you I loved you."

She smiled then. A bright, pure smile of happiness that nearly blinded him.

"I love you, too. I want to get free of my past so I can have a future with you. If you want me. I mean if you were talking about more than just a—"

He pulled her close and kissed her. Their lips met in a hot, hungry kiss that spoke of too much time apart and a lifetime of possibilities together.

"I was talking about forever," he said against her mouth. "I want to marry you." He chuckled. "If for no other reason than the minister is going to be saying your name out loud for the world to hear."

"I don't mind," she said, clinging to him. "Oh, Quinn, if you want you can join my business. We could expand and rescue more kids and maybe take on different projects. We could—"

He silenced her with another kiss. There would be plenty of time for business talk and details later. Right now he just wanted to be with the woman he loved.

"I can't believe I found you," he said as he touched the smooth leather over her back.

"I found you, remember? That day in the woods. I captured you."

He smiled. "Yes, you did. All of me." He dropped his hands to her hips. "So is there any sleazy lingerie on under this dress?"

"Sorry, no." She kissed him. "There isn't any underwear at all."

He groaned. "You're my kind of woman."

Daisy Jane Monroe shivered with pleasure at

those words. She'd come a long way toward healing, and she knew that all the pain and fear of her past was finally behind her. She'd learned to love enough to let go, and to hold on.

Quinn's woman. That was exactly who she wanted to be. He would be her man and together they would love each other for the rest of their lives.

* * * * *

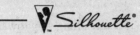

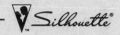

SPECIAL EDITION™

WINCHESTER
BRIDES

A WINCHESTER HOMECOMING
Pamela Toth
(Silhouette Special Edition #1562)

Heading home to Colorado to nurse her wounds seemed
like a good plan. But the newly divorced Kim Winchester
hadn't counted on running headlong into her childhood
sweetheart. The one-time rebel has become a seriously
handsome rancher—the kind of temptation love-wary Kim
would do *anything* to avoid.

Available September 2003 at your favorite retail outlet.

It's romantic comedy with a kick
(in a pair of strappy pink heels)!

Introducing

HARLEQUIN®
flipside

"It's chick-lit with the romance and happily-ever-after ending that Harlequin is known for."
—*USA TODAY* bestselling author Millie Criswell, author of *Staying Single,* October 2003

"Even though our heroine may take a few false steps while finding her way, she does it with wit and humor."
—Dorien Kelly, author of *Do-Over,* November 2003

Launching October 2003.
Make sure you pick one up!

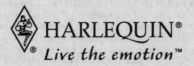

HARLEQUIN®
Live the emotion™

Visit us at www.harlequinflipside.com

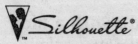

COMING NEXT MONTH

SPECIAL EDITION